The Sycamore Slopes

STACEY WEEKS

CHASED BY GRACE · CHANGED BY LOVE

Grace and Love Publishing

Cover image from unsplash: christine-donaldson-LSmzsqnJUmA-
unsplash.jpg

ISBN: 978-1-7387413-0-4

Grace and Love Publishing

Free Short Story

Download at StaceyWeeks.com

When sweet peppers and jalapeño mix, anything can happen.

Addison avoids visiting the city. He hates the crowds, traffic, and pace. He especially hates the compact vehicle the rental company insists he'd reserved. But then he runs into Sarah. Or, more accurately, she runs into him, mixing sweet peppers and jalapeño with burnt metal, petrol, hot pavement, and her desperation to not merely survive life in the city but find a place to thrive. Addison isn't looking for a weekend thrill or a romantic entanglement anymore than she is. They both want to go home. Maybe, together, they'll find their way.

Praise for The Sycamore Standoff

Weeks is a writer I count on for sweet contemporary romances with faith messages to make me think. Sycamore Standoff combines sympathetic characters with heartening takeaways about the freedom of living in grace and the power of community.

— AUTHOR EMILY CONRAD

The town of Sycamore Hill is warm and welcoming. The heart of God shines throughout the story. I really enjoyed The Sycamore Stand Off.

— JULIA - BOOK REVIEWER, CHRISTIAN BOOKAHOLIC

One of the things I enjoy about Stacey Weeks' writing is her ability to present a powerful & touching gospel message organic to the story, without it feeling forced or preachy. Instead of stopping an entertaining story for a sermon, Weeks uses the faith-centered elements to enhance the characters' journeys on the page and point to the Source of peace, strength, and courage.

— CARRIE ~ BOOK REVIEWER, READING IS MY SUPERPOWER

More Fiction by Stacey Weeks

To God, who has done far more for me than I could ask for or imagine.

So, whether you eat or drink, or whatever you do,
do all to the glory of God.

1 Corinthians 10:31

Contents

Chapter One

A bloodcurdling shriek sliced through the air. Ben Sawyer didn't flinch. He merely lifted his camera, peered through the lens, and rotated the focusing ring. He concentrated on Sycamore Hill's ice-covered pond, the origin of the happy squeals. Skaters glided into the frame, and he held down the shutter release to utilize the camera's continuous shooting mode—a trick a fellow reporter taught him. Small-town newspapers didn't have the budget for photographers. The reporters pulled double duty.

Local Kids Glide Toward Better Health. Not the best headline, but it'd have to do. The assignment editor threw this at Ben last minute. He thought an article on the town's outdoor activities paired well with Ben's exposé on the rising statistics of childhood obesity. Ben captured another cluster of images. The story wasn't a lead. Not even a shocker. It might as well be printed in the classifieds.

A chilly breeze pushed the scent of hot chocolate and corn dogs from a cluster of nearby food trucks. The sweet aroma dominated over sweaty bodies stuffed into winter snow suits. *Pop Up Food Vendors. Who Moderates Them?* Still boring, but he committed the potential headline to memory anyway.

Ben adjusted the camera lens again. The nip in the air reddened noses and chapped cheeks, but it colored no one more adorably than little Oliver, Kim Jansen's son. Kim had only recently regained custody of Oliver after her ex had spirited him out of the country. Ben covered the mother/son reunion for the paper, which was spearheaded by Oliver's Uncle Jackson.

Kim and Jackson sandwiched Oliver, clutching his mittened hands and supporting him on his skates. The average person would never guess all they had endured to get to this happy spot. But that's the way it often was. People only saw the outside. Scars lived underneath.

The blades slipped and slid beneath the boy. Oliver's face scrunched as if he were trying to climb Mount Everest. "I do it! I do it!"

Ben snapped another picture. *Local Boy Learns to Skate.* Cute kids dominated the front pages of Sycamore Hill's paper. This one was sure to score Ben a place above the fold, but it was hardly the exclusive that jump-started a career. He'd already written that exclusive, and it had gotten him nowhere.

A rope of kids linked hands to play crack the whip on the far side of the pond. Janelle Holmes, his neighbors' kid, squealed. The momentum of the skaters pulled the unfortunate tail over the surface of the ice.

Ben pivoted again. He zoomed in on the adjacent slope. Calling it a slope was a bit of a stretch, but it was the closest thing to a sledding hill the town could offer. Children slogged up the gentle incline, dragging sleds and plastic carpets behind them. Their friends zipped down the steep side in a strange conveyer belt of activity. He captured another grouping of images. *Fun on the Sycamore Slopes*. That should be enough.

But not Pulitzer Prize enough.

He navigated through the pictures, zooming in on faces, deleting the ones with closed eyes or unflattering angles. People liked seeing their photos in the paper, but only if their likeness complimented them. And parents loved seeing their children in print. He had enough shots of delighted youngsters for his bland assignment. Done with a capital D.

He repacked his satchel and squinted against the early pangs of a headache. The boughs of a frost-dusted pine tree blurred as he rubbed the butt of his palm in circles on his forehead. Could a career reporting for Sycamore News make him happy? Just the idea of covering common occurrences for the rest of his life made his limbs heavy. Everything required an astronomical effort. Even his lungs resisted inflating.

"Uncle Ben!" Nico waved as he raced toward the hill.

A long blue sled attached to a thin yellow rope bounced behind him.

The iceberg in his chest liquified. This was why he stayed. He wanted to watch his nephew grow up. He wanted to help his sister, Claire. He wanted to be here for his parents. But mostly, he wanted to make things permanent with Emma. He had the ring hidden in his bedside table. All he needed now was a plan. Nobody *just proposed* anymore.

"Look out!"

The panicked cry lifted the head of every adult. Ben swung, fumbling for his camera. Never pack the camera! Rookie mistake.

Powerful momentum sent Janelle on a trajectory toward Oliver. The ten-year-old girl's impact forced Oliver from Jackson and Kim's grip in seemingly slow motion. The boy catapulted into the air like a bull's prey and came down even harder with a thwack.

Silence fell just as spectacularly. Too quiet. Oliver should be crying.

No, no, no. No. NO.

This kind of quiet screamed everything was not okay. It roared in Ben's ears. Everything was not fine. Everything might never be fine again. His cold fingers fumbled for his phone. Emma was the top of his favorites. He stabbed the screen.

Emma didn't answer.

Come on. He tried again.

Still no answer.

He called a third time, knowing three calls in quick succession would override her silence feature.

"Hello?"

"Come to the slopes! There's been an accident."

That's all she needed. She promised to hurry.

Ben pushed through the cluster of people. He stuffed the phone into his zippered pocket. His fat fingers couldn't pull the tab to close the teeth.

Jackson's hands roamed each of Oliver's limbs, and Kim cradled Oliver's head, not moving his neck.

Janelle had crumpled onto the ice off to the side. Her elbows pressed into her body. "I'm sorry! I'm sorry!"

"Emma's on her way." Ben dropped to a knee beside Jackson. "She'll be here any second."

The tendons in Jackson's neck popped out as he nodded. "Keep his head stabilized, Kim."

As the only police presence in town, Jackson, with his emergency training, was the next best thing to Emma. And as the only nurse practitioner in a town with no doctors, Emma was the next best thing to a paramedic or hospital. Ben's fisted hand bounced against his thigh. She should be here by now.

Oliver roused. He tried to move.

Ben craned his neck to scan the line of parked cars on the side road, looking for Emma's familiar hatchback. *Come on.*

Kim leaned over Oliver so he could see her face. "Stay

still, baby. You'll be okay." Oliver's knitted red hat absorbed Kim's tears.

Ben smeared the sweat beading on his lips across his cheeks. Traumas that involved children— They changed you. He sucked in and held his breath.

Stop thinking about that.

Kim pressed her lips to Oliver's forehead, still stabilizing him and murmuring soft words.

She sounded just like his mother had.

Emma's medical bag thudded onto the ice beside Ben, jolting him from the past. He didn't even remember kneeling beside the boy, but his pant legs were soaked through. Emma checked Oliver's vitals. Her slender fingers moved his body. A long auburn braid fell over one shoulder, and her knitted toque had been knocked askew. The bright striped pattern of blue and red contrasted with her creamy skin. Her clear eyes fixed on Oliver. "How long was he out?"

Kim's features pinched. "Just a few minutes."

Seemingly satisfied that nothing was broken, Emma flicked a tiny penlight across Oliver's eyes. What she saw must have pleased her. As the stiffness in her posture loosened, Ben's relief shot out like a bullet.

Emma held Kim's gaze. "I think he'll be fine, but I'd like to take him to the clinic for a more thorough check up."

Kim wiped her eyes and reached for Jackson with a shaky hand. "Thank you."

"Can I carry him?" Jackson hovered, ready to scoop

the boy up but unwilling to move him until Emma gave the okay.

She nodded.

Jackson tenderly carried the child to Kim's van. Jackson was one of the good guys. The kind of police officer children could trust. Like the one that returned Ben to his parents when he was lost as a child.

Not like the other officer. Not like the one that took him away. Ben stretched his cramped fingers, flexing them at his sides.

Ben caught words and phrases like *champ, be brave, you'll be okay,* and *I've got you.* Jackson's optimistic tone and word choices contrasted with his sickly white complexion. The man loved that kid like a father.

"What took so long?" Ben shuffled closer to Emma as her attention shifted to Janelle.

Janelle's hands jammed into her armpits, and she rocked back and forth. Shallow breath sounds. Catatonic gaze.

Emma flicked her gaze to Ben, but instead of bouncing back to Janelle, she lingered. "I couldn't find a place to park." Her chin lifted to the right, and her head tilted. "Are you okay? You look pale."

Ben flattened his lips. The parking situation had become ridiculous. The pond and the slope jetted off a dead-end street. Vehicles filled the nearby side roads, many of them blocking the resident's driveways. "I'll be fine. But Janelle's not looking so good."

Emma knelt in front of Janelle. She patiently waited

for Janelle to lift her head. The circumference of the dark circle growing over Emma's denim-clad knees increased. She kept her hands still.

Finally, Janelle made eye contact.

"Are you hurt?"

Janelle shook her head. "Is Oliver gonna be okay?"

"I think so. How are you?"

Janelle blinked. At some point, her hat had fallen off, and static electricity lifted strands of her dark hair.

"I'm fine." Janelle cut her eyes to Ben. "Is this going to be in the paper?"

He started to say no but stopped. He'd been sent to report on the activities. The editor might divert to winter safety once he heard of the accident. "I don't know. But I won't take your picture unless you want me to." That, he could promise.

"I don't."

Ben patted his satchel. "Then my camera stays put."

"Can I check you over?" Emma placed a gentle hand on Janelle's shoulder.

Emma's soft mannerisms had a calming effect. Ben's erratic pulse normalized. Emma was not the doctor that made a terrible mistake. Jackson was not the police officer that took Ben away from his parents. Everything was going to be fine.

Janelle tugged her jacket sleeves down over her gloved hands. "I'm okay."

"I expect you are, but I'd like to be sure. Sometimes shock stops us from feeling everything."

Janelle nodded a curt consent.

Emma completed a basic examination and then sat back on her heels. "You're right. You seem fine. But I'll call your parents so they can keep an eye on you."

Janelle diverted her gaze.

Interesting. Was she afraid they'd be angry at her? Ben had never seen or heard anything concerning from his neighbor's house.

Emma repacked her emergency medical kit and hoisted herself to her feet. Her damp knees didn't seem to bother her. "I better get to the clinic. Oliver will be waiting."

Ben clutched the top of his satchel to camouflage the shakiness in his hands. "You have to fill out an incident report, right?"

She nodded.

"I saw the accident. It wasn't Kim or Jackson's fault. I want to add my testimony to the paperwork."

A tiny laugh bubbled from Emma. Not a laugh of mockery. She wasn't the type to poke fun. It was more like a chuckle of relief. She started to walk toward the side road where she must have parked, although he still couldn't see her vehicle. "That's not necessary. I'll make a note it was an ice-skating accident. It's no big deal."

Ben didn't remember the doctor's exact words to his mother, but they were probably similar and spoken in the same casual tone. The doctor had no idea that his belief in the system would rip Ben's family apart. Emma stood at the edge of the same cliff, and another family teetered on the precipice. "It's a big deal for me. I want to be sure everything is noted. You know, for later, if necessary."

Emma stopped and faced Ben, fisting her hands on her hips. Her eyebrows pulled together, and her nose wrinkled adorably. "Did something happen that you're not telling me?"

He avoided her eyes. He wasn't ready. He might never be ready. "If you have legal responsibilities to report certain types of injuries, I just want to be there."

She studied him for a second longer before conceding. "You're a sweet man for caring so much." She lifted onto her tiptoes and pressed a chaste kiss to his lips.

An unexpected release of tension loosened the knots in Ben's neck. He wasn't sure whether it was relief over not needing to explain why this mattered so much or her yielding to his request. But either way, justice would prevail.

"Thank you. I'll be there as soon as I can." He lightly squeezed her hands as she pulled away.

She gave him a playful wink. "Don't be long."

Now the excitement was over, skaters had returned to the ice. They twirled and held hands. Blades scraped the frozen surface, mixing with laughter and innocent squealing. Life went on.

Someone pressed play on their winter playlist, but it couldn't quite smother the songs of childhood. Ben wanted this for his kids. A community. A place to belong. A place that stood together.

His future kids.

An increasing warmth in his chest warred with his cold toes. Emma had reached her car, tucked between two vans. She turned for a final wave, disappeared inside, and drove off. He and Emma hadn't discussed children yet. They discussed marriage. That was where their track headed. At least it was where he hoped it was headed. They'd reached what his mom called "the ripe age of early thirties," and according to her, their train raced to the tick of a biological clock.

His career ran alongside that train on a parallel track. At least, it was parallel until Grander City Daily News offered him a job. It wasn't the hard-hitting journalism he once dreamed of, but it was a step up from Sycamore Hill. The only catch was they required him to move to the city. Emma had worked too hard to become a nurse practitioner and open her medical clinic to follow him to the city. He'd have to choose.

He'd worked his whole life for an opportunity to report at a big city paper and stir the poisonous pots the government had its hands in. But now that a paper had reached out, his feet got cold. Ben stomped his boots, and they sunk into the snow. A frosty tingle crept toward his ankles.

He couldn't think about that right now. Protecting Oliver was all that mattered. The poor kid had already suffered enough in his young life. Ben would write an article that mentioned the incident. It ensured the truth was officially recorded somewhere. It was an accident. And someone other than the doctor and police needed to know.

Accidents happened. This wasn't anybody's fault.

Chapter Two

"I'll be a few more minutes with Oliver, then I'll take a closer look at Janelle."

Janelle's mother, Kellie Holmes, nodded her head. Her mousy brown hair fell forward. "Thank you."

Kellie's words, tone, and facial expression conveyed appropriate emotion, but her demeanor didn't quite match. Emma's belly somersaulted. Something was amiss. She made a short note on the appointment chart at her reception desk.

The clinic's exterior door slammed against the door stopper. Ben stumbled in, and the door bounced back into place. His spectacular entrance drew every eye, but it was Janelle's wince that made her curious.

Ben's gaze roamed the reception area as he tugged off his cap. Short tufts of dark hair sprung to attention. "Is Oliver okay? Have you signed off on his injuries?" His words huffed with each rise and fall of his chest.

Did the man run all the way here?

"He's fine." Emma walked around the desk. "Kim and Jackson are with him now. Are you okay?" She squinted as she stared into his eyes. She always loved Ben's dark eyes, but this moment had nothing to do with romance. His pupils constricted. It was probably due to the brightly-lit waiting room. She led Ben to the nearest chair.

"I had to run here. My car was blocked in."

That explained his heaving chest and flushed complexion. But what explained the panic? She dispensed some cooler water into a tiny paper cup and handed it to him.

Ben looked like he was about to say something more, but he closed his mouth and accepted the cup.

She let his erratic behavior go. She had a patient in the room, another in the queue, and a receptionist who'd called in sick.

"Is Oliver really okay?" Ben studied her as if trying to read her non-verbal cues.

"Kim and Jackson can fill you in." She wouldn't divulge detailed patient information. Ben's concern might be genuine, but the ethical line existed for a reason.

Jackson poked his head out from the examination area. "Is that Ben?" When his gaze landed on his friend, he briefly disappeared behind the door before popping out again, pulling the door closed behind him. He extended his hand to Ben. "Kim and Oliver are fine. We really appreciate your concern. Emma told us how important it was to you that everything was documented properly."

Ben shook Jackson's hand.

"I'll wait here with you." Jackson claimed the empty seat next to Ben. "Did you catch the game last night?"

Emma threw Jackson a thankful nod and then hurried back to her patient.

"Ben sure is sweet." Kim stroked her fingers through Oliver's hair. It was still baby fine, and her movements sent several strands to attention.

Emma closed the door behind her.

Sweet. That was one way to describe it. Another word was relentless. A dog with a bone. His tenacity was what made him a good reporter.

"I'm going to test your reflexes, Oliver. Is that okay?"

The boy's eyes expanded when she pulled her reflex hammer from her pocket. He burrowed his face into Kim's side.

Emma chuckled. She tapped the hammer. "It's got a soft head. Want to feel it?"

Oliver peeked from behind a fold of fabric and nodded. Oliver was one month shy of his third birthday.

Emma extended the hammer, and he reached out a tentative hand and stroked its head.

"I'll tap your knee, and it should bounce. See?" Emma tested Oliver's deep tendon reflex, and the boy giggled as his leg gave an involuntary kick.

"I didn't know Ben cared so much about the kids in

the community." Kim rubbed small circles into Oliver's back. "It's kind."

Sure. They'd use that word. Kind.

Not overbearing.

Not disproportionate.

"Now, we'll check your coordination. First, I'd like you to put your hands on your thighs."

Oliver looked at his mom.

"These are your thighs." Kim tapped Oliver's quadriceps.

He complied.

"Turn your hands over and lift them up." Emma modelled the action.

Oliver completed the task. "This is silly."

Emma grinned. "If you think this is silly, try doing it over and over as fast as you can."

A belly laugh rumbled deep within Oliver, and the sound made Emma's heart swell. He was going to be just fine.

"You're great with kids."

Emma thanked the Lord Kim's eyes stayed on Oliver. Judging from the temperature in her cheeks, they had to be blazing red. "Thanks."

"How long have you and Ben been dating?"

Emma bounced her gaze back to Oliver. "About a year."

"Hmmmm." The sound wasn't even a word, yet it carried a punch.

"We had our first date at last year's Life House

banquet."

Kim perked up at the mention of the gala. She'd organized the annual fundraiser that brought in enough money to support Life House and its ministries for the following year.

Emma twisted her lips to the side. "Did I ever tell you how we ended up attending together?" She lifted Oliver from the examination table and set his feet on the floor.

Oliver reached out as if he were about to touch the stethoscope slung around Emma's neck. Kim wagged a finger at him, and he retracted his hand.

"It's a funny story. Ben literally broke through my skylight the night before your event."

"You're kidding."

"Right through the ceiling and onto my kitchen floor." She shifted her gaze back to Kim's son. "Now I want you to touch your nose. Can you do that?"

"How come *that* never made the paper?"

"It did, in a way. He was chasing a lead for the Emergence story. That's how I got involved. By the time we cleaned up the mess the broken skylight had created, he'd invited me to attend the gala with him."

Oliver pressed his index fingertip to his nose. One digit slipped inside, and Kim gently tugged his arm to pull it out. She made a face at him. "That's gross."

Emma had been about to ask Oliver if he could touch her fingertip with his, but she twisted around and grabbed a hand wipe from the back counter instead. She disinfected Oliver's fingers and tossed the wipe in the trash. She stretched out her index finger. "Now, touch my finger with your fingertip."

Oliver pressed his fingertip to hers.

"Now touch your nose."

He obeyed.

"And my finger. And your nose. Keep doing this."

As Oliver alternated between touching his nose and Emma's finger, Kim peppered Emma with questions. "Is Ben always this intense around kids? Did he ask for your help in the Emergence trial? Why is he so wound up about Oliver's skating accident? I appreciate his concern for Oliver, but . . ." her voice trailed off.

"That's good, Oliver," Emma deflected. "Now close your eyes and see if you can keep touching your nose and my finger. No peeking."

The boy giggled.

Emma didn't know how to answer Kim. The way Ben pressed Emma to document everything was a bit offensive. Emma knew how to do her job, but she sensed there was more to the story.

"Good job, Oliver. Open your eyes. Now, let's see if you can repeat the experiment with the other hand."

Ben's restlessness concerned her. He was overreacting, that was for sure. Kids get hurt. And despite Ben's assurance that he knew that, his actions told a different story.

"One more test, Oliver, then we'll be all done. You're doing great."

"Do you ever think about having kids?"

Kim's question twanged Emma's heart. She tried to set her thoughts aside, but they fought back. She used to assume she would have kids, and then school took up all her time, then starting the clinic. But once she'd met Ben, and she began to hope that maybe, one day, the Lord would answer her prayer for a family.

Kim must have read something in her expression because she pulled back. "I'm sorry. That was nosy of me."

Emma smiled. "It's okay. Oliver, can you walk from this trolley cart to the edge of the curtain and back again?"

"What are you checking for?"

"Gait. How he walks and swings his arms tells me a lot." Emma had Oliver repeat the test on his toes, walking heel to toe, on his heels, and finally, she had him hop in place.

"Oliver will be fine. If he has a headache, over the counter pain medication should be sufficient. If you have any other concerns, or anything new develops, just give me a call." She retrieved Oliver's jacket from the wall hook and handed it to Kim, placing the matching snow pants on the examination table.

"Thanks, Emma. I'm really thankful you opened your clinic. Sycamore Hill needed local medical care." Kim stuffed one little, wiggly arm into the puffy coat and started wrestling with the other.

Emma was thankful, too. Running her own clinic was a dream come true. She opened a cupboard and pulled out a small trunk shaped like a treasure box. She'd stuffed it with all sorts of goodies. Emma opened the lid and held it out to Oliver. "You did such a great job. Why don't you pick a prize from my prize box?"

Oliver freed his arm from the jacket sleeve as he reached for the box. His gaze flicked to his mom's, and she nodded. He dipped his hand into the treasure and rooted around, removing several options to examine them.

"He doesn't need any imaging?" Kim asked.

"It's not necessary, but if you'd feel better, I can order some."

"No, that's okay. If you're satisfied, so am I."

Oliver still debated his prize choice.

"It's a tough decision, isn't it?"

His lips puckered. He scrunched his forehead. "I want the bubbles."

"Good choice," Kim affirmed.

After wiping down the equipment and changing the paper that covered the examination table, Emma followed Kim and Oliver to the waiting room. How Oliver tucked his hand into his mother's and looked up at her with such adoration intensified Emma's longing for a family of her own. Kim fought hard to get here—to get Oliver back from her ex. Hayden might have gotten away with the parental abduction had his twin brother, Jackson, not intervened.

And now Jackson was here with Kim, and they made a beautiful family.

One day, Lord willing, she'd have one too. A family. Her eyes sought Ben. If she kept saying one day, would she eventually run out of days?

Ben was just as career-driven as she was, especially after breaking the Emergence story. When no immediate offers came from the big papers after the exclusive hit the news, he deflated. She loved Ben, and she wanted good things for him. But if an offer came in from a larger paper, he'd have to move. And her clinic was here, in Sycamore Hill. She bit the inside of her cheek. What if she wasn't enough reason for him to stay?

Oliver tugged free of his mother and darted into Jackson's outstretched arms. "Look, Unca Jackson. Bubbles!"

"We'll have fun with those."

Jackson, Kim, and Oliver left, and Emma wondered how long it would be before they announced wedding plans. Oliver's biological dad might be Jackson's deadbeat brother, but it was obvious to anyone who saw the threesome that they made a perfect family. But they had baggage.

But who didn't? She and Ben lugged an entire luggage set.

Ben slumped in his chair.

"Janelle can go into the examination room," Emma said to Kellie. "I'll be right there."

Kellie motioned for Janelle to move, and the girl hopped to her feet.

Emma frowned. Janelle moved more gingerly than

she had at the pond. Had she missed something in her initial examination? Was it a simple case of the aches settling in?

"You wrote everything down, right?"

Ben's fixation made her jaw tense. A bee was having a fit in his bonnet. "Of course, I wrote everything down."

Their gazes held for a long minute. There was something Ben wasn't telling her. Before she could probe deeper, Ben's sister, Claire, burst through the clinic doors with Ben's nephew, Nico. "Help!"

Chapter Three

Ben bolted to his sister and slipped his arm under Nico to help support his weight. Claire transferred Nico's weight to Ben. How did she get the boy this far on her own? The ten-year-old was solid. Built like a linebacker. A tank. At the moment, a very wobbly tank with bones of jelly.

"Lay him down." Emma directed them to a second examination room with a table.

Ben scooped Nico under his knees and arms and carried him to the bed. The white sheets amplified the paleness of Nico's usually warm skin tone.

"He was on the hill." Claire wrapped her arms around her middle. "His sled hit a tree."

Nico was conscious but groggy. "Uncle Ben?" His eyelids fluttered.

Ben's knees weakened. "That's a good sign, right?"

"Did he lose consciousness?" Emma's tone had

shifted from the slightly irritated woman bothered by Ben's questions to a focused, in-command professional.

Ben sagged. *Thank you, God, for Emma.*

"Briefly." Claire's voice caught. She pressed a fist into her mouth. His sister. His only sister. A sister he might not have known had things played out differently. The trickle-down effect of the possible paths his life could have taken hit like a sledgehammer. If he didn't know Claire, he wouldn't know his brother-in-law. He'd have never met Nico.

Stop.

Ben wrapped an arm around Claire's shoulder and pulled her into a side hug. She slumped into him. "He'll be okay. Emma will take care of him."

Claire turned into him. A quiet sob rippled down her frame. "It was awful. He wouldn't open his eyes. I keep seeing it over and over in slow motion, and there is nothing I can do to stop it."

Lord, have mercy.

"Nico, can you tell me where you are?" Emma hovered over Nico so they were eyeball to eyeball. Her intensity iced Ben's veins. She was probably checking to see if his pupils responded the same or if they were unequal, but fear nearly took him out at the knees.

"Doctor's."

"That's good." Emma smiled. "Who am I?"

"Auntie Emma."

Ben melted. Lord willing, one day, she'd *really* be

Nico's Auntie Emma, and the title would be more than an endearment.

Emma flicked a glance at her watch and refocused on Nico. She was secretly taking his pulse. Ben had been around her long enough to recognize her tricks for monitoring her patients. "Do you have a headache?"

Nico peeked at Emma through tightly squeezed lids. Ben usually joked about the boy's stocky build, but right now, all he could think was how fragile God had made the human body. How delicate life was. How quickly it could be gone.

Changed.

His throat narrowed. He swallowed, but thickness made it nearly impossible.

"A little."

"That's to be expected. You have quite the bump starting. Are you dizzy?"

"Not anymore."

"Is the light bothering you?" Emma gestured to the bright overhead fluorescents.

"No."

Emma was running through a checklist, looking for clues as to whether Nico had a concussion. Each question landed with the force of a fist on his gut. This wasn't just any kid. This was Nico. His nephew. His responsibility.

And Ben didn't take that lightly.

While Claire's husband was deployed overseas, protecting the family fell to Ben. He and Matt had an arrangement. Matt defended the country, and Ben supported the family.

Emma started running Nico through the same drill she imposed upon every patient who presented with a possible head injury.

Notes. He should be taking notes. Ben pulled out his phone and opened the note app. "Claire, tell me exactly what happened."

"I don't know. I was chatting with Gloria, and one of Nico's friends came to get me."

Ben groaned. That wouldn't be sufficient for the courts. Without details, history might repeat itself. God wouldn't allow something so cruel.

Except maybe He would.

Because He had.

Nothing occurred that God hadn't allowed. Not even this. The theology of God's sovereignty during tragedy rose like a hurdle Ben wasn't sure he could clear. Not when it involved Nico. Not when he knew how bad things could get. "Think!"

"Ben," Emma cut in like a fresh breeze in the desert. Ben's internal temperature had doubled since Claire arrived with Nico in her arms, but Emma's calm tone and clear-headedness fell like sweet spring rain.

"Take a breath before I have to stop treating Nico and come treat you." Her busy hands had stilled. They all stared at him, but it was Emma's gaze he held onto.

Her forehead puckered. It drew her eyebrows together in a question. His expression? He wasn't sure.

But based on her reaction and how hot his face felt, he'd have to guess wild-eyed.

Ben closed his eyes and forced himself to inhale deeply. *Whatever the day holds, Lord, I want to trust you.*

Ben wasn't some fair-weather Christian that only accepted good from God's hand. He was realistic. God owed them nothing. But he also knew the real injuries could hit long after the body healed, coming from nowhere. A man could do everything right and still have everything go wrong at the hands of the very people dedicated to protecting life and health.

He knew because he'd lived it.

So had Claire, but she didn't remember as he did. She'd been too young.

Seemingly satisfied with Ben's response, Emma pivoted to Claire. "Nico seems to be okay. I want to keep him here for a bit. In ten minutes, I'll run through the tests again, and then one more time in thirty minutes, just to be sure. Assuming everything comes back fine, I'll send you home with some concussion protocols."

"Protocols?"

"Basic stuff. His brain needs to rest."

"If he falls asleep, do I wake him up?"

"No, not if I determine he's fine. Over-the-counter pain medications for the headache and complete rest for the first twenty-four hours should be sufficient as long as nothing new surfaces. If he doesn't rest like he needs to, the recovery is much longer." Emma rested a gentle hand on Claire's upper arm. "I'll print it all out for you. And I promise you, I'll take good care of him."

"I know you will." Claire's eyes dampened as she shuffled closer to Nico.

Ben locked eyes with Emma. Emma loved them. She wouldn't put anything on that chart to jeopardize his family. He believed that with everything in him. But sometimes, that didn't matter. Sometimes a person higher up made a decision you could do nothing about.

He believed that, too.

Hours later, after Ben had settled Nico at home and Claire had assured him that she was okay, Ben headed to the office. He still had a deadline to meet.

"Ben, I need you to swing by the condo site this week and speak with Franklin Cooper about the delays." Thomas leaned his hip against the side of Ben's desk.

"Did we get another complaint?"

"Another letter to the editor. Seems like the neighborhood folk are getting tired of staring at mounds of dirt all day."

Ben wasn't surprised. New Horizon Properties tore down the only four houses in Sycamore Hill's historic area that were not historic homes. They started work on the condos in the summer. Their design plan indicated the new builds would match the neighborhood, but there were a lot of unhappy people when it first hit the news. "I thought we'd milked that cow already?"

"We did, but my contact in Grander City said that Cooper's taken a financial hit on a few other builds that will delay finishing this one. Take a look at this." He handed Ben a printout.

Ben scanned it. This was not going to go over well with the community. They could be staring at a mound of dirt downtown for months.

Thomas handed him another piece of paper. Thomas was probably the only person on earth that still preferred actual paper to electronic notes.

"What's this?"

"It's another letter about the slopes. I think it's referring to Nico."

Nico? Ben snapped the page in his hand. Thomas had printed an email that came through shortly after Nico's accident.

The children's use of our town's slopes and pond has become quite a nuisance for our neighborhood. I understand kids need to play, but recent injuries have compelled me to speak up.

Two children were injured today, one skating and one sledding. I understand accidents happen, and children can't grow up in a protective bubble, but the slopes and pond are dangerous and relatively unsupervised. We are lucky the injuries weren't worse.

The town needs to close access to the slopes and pond for the sake of our children or invest in moderating them better. It's high time the authorities stepped up to protect our children.

A Concerned Citizen.

Conflicting emotions tore through Ben, but he fought to keep them off his face. Local parents should be able to decide whether their kids could skate or sled. There was no way Ben wanted the authorities poking their noses in where they didn't belong. Parents parented, not the government. And he knew better than anyone what happened when someone on a power trip took on the role of protector.

But a small part of him, a tiny voice that he couldn't seem to shut off, agreed with the anonymous writer. Or at least he saw the person's point. The slopes were dangerous. Nico did get hurt. And it could have been much worse. Closing the slopes meant no injuries, which meant there was no need for the authorities to investigate individual families. Was it possible that allowing over-reach in one area would protect them from a deeper and more dangerous reach in another?

"What do you think?" Thomas folded his arms across his chest. "Is this inviting the authorities to exercise power they shouldn't have? Who gets to decide what kids do on public land? Who knows what's best for kids, parents, or the community? This is your wheelhouse."

Ben's passion to cut overreaching arms at the elbows and expose corrupt authorities should have dusted this assignment in catnip, but it hit too close to home. He'd debate any other topic. He'd write about anything else. But not this. Not this time. Not when it had the potential to blow back on his family.

"I'm running the letter." Thomas eyed him carefully.

Ben dropped it on his desk. If Thomas caught a whiff of Ben's internal struggle, he'd give the story to someone else. Someone who might not do it justice. Someone who'd make things worse. "How can you run it without his name?" He kept his voice non-committal. Neutral. Switzerland.

Thomas snickered. "He might have signed it that way, but he sent it from his personal email. The letter came from Hank Sinclair. I already spoke with Hank, and he admitted to writing it and agreed to have his name attached to it. I want you to follow up with Hank."

The liquid in Ben's veins froze. This was headed for disaster. He could feel it, like a cold hand on his spine. Good ol' Hank. Older than Moses and impossible to please. The man stirred the pot at so many church meetings that Ben would have stopped attending them if the paper didn't require his presence. The guy was a hornet, willing to sting unprovoked.

"What letter?" A waft of rosewater drifted from behind.

Emma.

She dropped a sweet kiss on Ben's cheek. "Sorry I'm late. I wanted to finish up the paperwork while things were still fresh. Then, Kathryn called to confirm our plans for lunch later this week."

Right. He and Emma scheduled a double date with Kathryn and Ethan. Emma and Kathryn had gotten to know each other better when Kathryn interviewed

Emma on her internet morning show for Emma's part in exposing the scoundrels at Emergence Pharmaceutical. The two had become fast friends.

"Hank Sinclair wrote the paper." Thomas answered. "He wants to shut down the slopes and the pond because of the incidents this morning."

"Really?" Emma's eyes widened. Her mouth curved into a smile. Not a disrespectful one, because despite how quick-witted Emma could be, she never mocked people. It was more of a shocked smile. Incredulous. A can-you-believe-some-people sort of smile. But when she turned to him, the smile died. "Do you agree with him, Ben?"

Shoot. His brain might not know how he felt, but his face did. He re-schooled his features into what he hoped was a more open expression. "I'm the press, so that makes me neutral. Just call me Switzerland."

"But you see how ridiculous this is, don't you?" Emma's head vacillated between Ben and Thomas, her long braid swinging with her. "They were accidents. Accidents can happen anywhere. If he wanted to log a legitimate complaint, it should be about the parking situation. I had to park more than a block away to get to the slopes."

Ben inhaled deeply through his nose. She was so innocent. It was one of the things he loved about her. The world hadn't jaded her yet. When his lips started to tingle, he unclenched his jaw. "Like I said, neutral."

Chapter Four

"Thanks for coming back in today." Emma welcomed Claire, Ben, and Nico from behind the clinic's reception desk. With her receptionist still out sick, Emma pulled triple duty, greeting and treating patients while answering the phones. She had been tempted to take Kathryn up on her offer to pinch hit as a receptionist, but thankfully, Nico was her last patient for the day.

Before they could respond, the shrill of the phone interrupted. Emma raised her index finger, indicating she needed a minute. "Emma Powles, Nurse Practitioner." While she made several notes in her calendar, adjusting an appointment for the caller, she watched the threesome covertly. They stood at reception, stiff, pale, and pinned under an elephant of unknowns. Interesting.

"Thank you for calling. I'll see you then." She disconnected and circled the desk. Claire's short dark hair, recently cut into a pixie style that flattered her heart-shaped face, usually made her blue eyes pop, but right now, concern darkened them. Emma wished she could alleviate Claire's deep-set anxiety, but Claire and Ben had circled the wagons and left Emma on the outside.

Claire wrung her hands.

Ben stood behind his sister, holding Nico's hand. His grip tightened when their gazes met, and the moisture in Emma's mouth evaporated. Every time Ben filled in for Matt as a stand-in parent, her midsection flip-flopped. This peek at the kind of father Ben could be, if the Lord blessed them with a future, threatened her heart. The more she hoped, the greater the risk of disappointment. The pessimistic route was safer. Yet, her cheeks warmed. She couldn't stop the lurch in her heart. Her thumb rubbed against the backside of the fourth digit on her ringless left hand. Nothing good came from running ahead of God.

Emma ruffled Nico's hair, but the boy pulled away, surly. The rejection landed like a blow. Wow, oh for three. She straightened, stiffened her lips, and slipped into her nurse persona. Professional. Detached. Safe.

"This is just a follow-up. Nothing concerning." She motioned for them to enter the examination room. Did Nico's sullenness stem from being unwell or being a preteen? She cut a glance to Ben. What was his excuse? She tugged on a thick curtain, and the metal rollers moved around the track, revealing an examination table. "Hop up, Nico."

He shrugged out of his winter coat and handed it to his mother. He jumped onto the table. His movements presented as normal and fluid. "How are you feeling?"

"Bored."

Preteen for the win.

Ben chuckled. With the laugh, his entire body relaxed, and the tight lines on his face eased. Whoever said laughter was the best medicine wasn't far from the truth. "This is the longest break he's ever had from his gaming system."

"Mom won't let me on *any* screen." Nico dragged the word *any* over three syllables and folded his arms across his chest.

"And yet, you've lived to tell the tale. A-ma-zing," Ben deadpanned, copying Nico's whiny tone.

Emma suppressed a smile. "Head injuries are tricky. It's better to be extra safe and do nothing for one whole day than do too much and then be off screens for months." Emma wiggled her eyebrows as if the possibility of such a long time without screens would be the worst thing in the world. Which it probably would be to a boy Nico's age.

Nico mumbled what sounded like agreement.

Emma picked up her tablet and opened her notes on Nico. "You had a headache yesterday. How is your head today?"

Nico shrugged.

"I gave him pain medication every six hours yesterday, but he hasn't had any since bedtime last night."

Claire's constant hand twisting projected more alarm than the situation warranted.

"Is your headache gone now, Nico?" His pupils looked good. Emma didn't see any indicators that rang an alarm.

"It don't hurt no more."

Emma made another note and then studied her would-be nephew. Would-be if Ben ever proposed.

"You can't be this upset about one day without your games." *And your mom can't be this upset about a simple fall.* "What gives?"

Nico flicked his gaze away.

Emma turned to Claire, who shrugged. "Got me. I've been asking all morning, and that's all I get."

"Nico, if something else is going on, you have to tell me." Emma rolled the stool from the computer terminal to the edge of the examination table and sat down. Nico perched on the edge of the bed, swinging his legs. She placed a hand near his knee, and his swinging stopped. "Nico?"

Their eyes met briefly. He turned away, but not before she saw the dampness in them. "The kids at school are mad."

A tiny crack in the circled wagons opened. "Mad you got hurt?"

"Mad that the slope and pond might get closed because I got hurt."

Emma bit the inside of her cheek. She and Ben hadn't discussed their opposing positions on this debate since their lunch date yesterday, where Ben finally confessed that he wasn't as neutral as he had claimed. Switzerland, her foot.

Ben had leaned toward closing things down *for the sake of the kids*. If they could do something to ensure the children's safety, why wouldn't they?

Emma hated that a stupid hill could divide them and trickle down to split others. All the way to a fifth grade classroom.

"Kathryn Withers was talking about it on her show this morning." Claire smoothed Nico's hair, but he pulled away. She dropped her hand to his shoulder.

Ben shot Nico a trenchant look.

Emma had worked too late finishing up paperwork to catch her friend's *Sycamore Hill at Sunrise* program. Kathryn often had the local scoop before the paper went to print. Most townfolk tuned in to catch her spin on resident gossip.

Claire squeezed Nico's shoulder. "Hank Sinclair is pushing pretty hard for the pond and slopes to close. Kathryn interviewed him. He cited the accidents yesterday as proof they weren't safe and said even if parents were present, they weren't watching their kids."

Claire's cheeks reddened, and Emma recalled her admittance that she didn't see the accident that caused Nico's injury because she was visiting with Gloria Sycamore.

"Kathryn's camera panned the side road, rolling footage from a previous day. The parking situation looked horrible. Especially with the food trucks taking up so much space. It was chaos."

"And everyone at school blames me," Nico grunted.

Emma narrowed her eyes. "How do you know if you didn't go back to school?"

A pink flush crept past the collar of his shirt.

"Did you use your phone?" Claire's voice rose.

The pink turned red, reaching his cheeks.

Emma clucked her tongue. "That wasn't a bright move, buddy. No screens means no screens."

Claire glared at her son. "We'll talk about this more at home." Her hardness softened when she shifted her gaze to Emma. "Hank started a petition to close off access to the area for the rest of the winter. It's gaining some traction, especially with the people who live in that neighborhood."

"And the kids blame you?" Ben, who'd remained quiet until now, squatted in front of Nico.

Nico stared at his feet, avoiding his uncle. "It's my fault for getting hurt."

"You didn't carve the path that led to the tree. It could have happened to any one of your friends."

Ben's logic wouldn't work on fifth graders.

"Besides, the controversy is probably more about the chaos the area brings to the neighborhood than it is about you. Emma couldn't find a spot to park anywhere close to the slopes. I had to walk here after the accident because my car was blocked. If the town clears that up, this problem all goes away."

Walk here? Emma snorted. Try sprint.

"Doesn't matter," Nico grumbled.

"What about Janelle?" Claire pressed. "Are they blaming her as well?"

He shrugged.

Emma gave her head a slight shake, and Claire dropped it, despite her hackles getting all mamma bearish.

Emma ran Nico through the same tests as yesterday, updating her notes on her tablet as they went along. "Nico seems to be recovering well."

Claire's stiffness relaxed. "His dad'll be relieved. It's hard to be away when things like this happen."

Matt was a sergeant with the Canadian Armed Forces. He had been tasked to help with training at Camp Aldershot in Nova Scotia, where he'd remain for another two months at least. Emma couldn't imagine Claire's life. It must be hard to have a husband on deployment and function as a single parent for many months, carrying the weight of every decision and managing the house. That's why Ben's presence mattered so much.

"Nico can gradually return to normal activities, starting slow and going to the next more active and mentally taxing activity if there continue to be no symptoms."

"That means no hockey tonight, buddy." Ben nudged his shoulder.

"Awwwwww." If Nico slumped any further, he'd

turn himself inside out. He folded his arms across his chest, and his bottom lip jutted out.

Ben tapped Nico's shoulder with a soft fist. "Why don't I pick you up after school, and you can come with me to interview Franklin Cooper."

Nico harrumphed. Double whammy. No screens or hockey, but well enough to go back to school. Poor kid.

"See if you can get Frank to tell you when the condos will be done." Claire handed Nico his jacket. "I'm tired of the dirt blowing from the build site. I had to clean my windows once a week until the cold finally came and froze it in place."

Emma's lips twitched at Nico's souring expression. He shoved his arms into his coat with the force of a torpedo. Interviewing a builder was not the carrot that would entice this horse.

"Afterward, I'll take you for chili cheese nachos."

Nico lifted his face.

There's the carrot.

"You know, Nico." Emma straightened some folders that didn't need straightening. "You could start your own petition. Something to challenge the grinch's position."

"The grinch?" Nico's voice lightened.

"Sounds like a grinch to me." Emma lifted a shoulder. Was that the beginning of a tiny smile?

It mattered to her that the kids had a place to play outside. Every winter, more and more children reverted to virtual activities instead of fresh air and exercise. They had more interaction with two-dimensional people than three. She wanted better for Nico. "Maybe you could seek the support of the Sycamore family? They are pretty invested in the town."

"I don't know," Claire interjected. "Hank already feels like that family gets preferential treatment."

"They do have a lot of influence on the council, but what's wrong with that? Hank's trying to influence the council. Besides, this is about the kids, not who's running the town."

"It's always about who's running the town," Ben added dryly. "But I don't know how wise it is to stir this pot. Hank wrote a second letter to the paper. Thomas didn't print it out of respect for us."

"Us?" Emma's eyes stretched.

"Claire and I."

The other us. Emma's cheeks burned. "What did he say?"

Ben's eyes shuttered. "Something about unexplainable injuries and protecting families from similar investigations to ours."

Claire's face drained of color. "How does he know?"

Unexplainable injuries? Investigations? Emma's mouth sagged. What injuries? How long ago were these injuries? Why would Hank bring this up as a defense for his position? She had so many questions. But as her head swirled from Ben to Claire, she snapped her jaw closed. Claire's sickly complexion and glassy eyes catapulted a new priority to the forefront.

"Sit here." Emma pushed a chair into the back of

Claire's knees to force her to sit before she fell over. She pressed a cup of cold water into her hand. Emma counted the pulse throbbing in her neck. "Drink this."

Claire's eyes cleared. "That's ancient history. We didn't even live here then. The charges were dropped." She lifted her chin, but it trembled. She spoke with more bravado than she projected. "What do you say, kiddo? Should we stop by the Sycamores' house and see what they think about this kerfuffle?"

"Yes!" Nico jumped from the examination table and punched a fist in the air.

"You still need to take it easy." Emma grinned.

Ben raked his fingers through his hair, the only one not sucked into the celebration. "I don't like this. If you go that route, the town will take sides, and this could blow up into a big deal. More than skating and sledding. And you'll be at the center."

"Seems to me like they are already at the center." Emma kept her eyes on Claire as she spoke.

Ben's frown deepened.

Did he really think that something as trivial as a sledding hill could divide a town, or was this somehow more connected to whatever happened to his family in the past? Nico's injury triggered something. Something Ben hadn't told her. Something he needed to tell her.

Ben's scowl constricted until his lips nearly disappeared.

"Emma's right," Claire said. "I bet Hank wants the place shut down because of the parking, noise, hot chocolate, and vendors. Their quiet cul-de-sac has become a carnival for half the year. That is what he wants to stop. If we address that, it all goes away."

Emma was right.

Ben glared at her.

She should have stayed neutral and claimed Switzerland.

Chapter Five

Ben picked up his pace. Being late for an interview screamed unprofessional, and a guy never knew when a scout watched. Sloppy little league players never got called to the majors. As he stepped off the curb, a car trying to squeeze into a space far too small leaned on the horn. He made a show of glancing at the no parking sign before making eye contact with the driver. *That's right. I see the sign you're ignoring.*

Vehicle congestion forced Ben to park more than a block away from Hank's house. By the time he'd slid into a spot and hoofed it there on foot, it would have been quicker for him to walk from the office.

Ben took the porch steps two at a time, noting how the back end of a compact vehicle blocked half of Hank's driveway. Ben could have pulled his car into the driveway if that one had not been illegally parked.

Hank swung open the front door before Ben could knock and barked, "You're late."

Ben shuffled back a step or two. The glare in the angry man's eyes told Ben all he needed to know about the straw that broke Hank's back. Or, to be more precise, the Honda Civic out front.

Noise from a television spilled from another room. Hank slashed his hand in a downward motion. "Let's get this over with."

Ben followed the man through the small entryway. Considering Hank's goal to sway people to his point of view, Ben expected a more cordial greeting.

But Hank was rarely cordial.

Hank jerked a thumb toward an armchair across from a worn recliner, and Ben sat down. "What prompted you to write that letter to the paper?" Ben had to practically yell to be heard over the news program.

"I already told you—" Hank stabbed a button on a remote control, and the TV went dark, "—those kids got hurt. It's about the kids."

A high-pitched carnival song replaced the newscast. The melody reminded Ben of the blare from an ice cream truck that got stuck in your head. It leaked through the seams of the closed windows on Hank's modest house and polluted the living room. Ben knew without looking that the music spilled from the hot chocolate and pretzel vendors near the middle of the expanse between the pond and the slopes. Their portable businesses left every night at dusk and set up again as soon as school let out on the weekdays and all day on Saturday. Sunday was the only day the vendors remained quiet.

But that wasn't likely to last much longer.

Ben had heard the song a thousand times while Nico sped down the slope, but he had never once considered how it fell on the people who lived here.

Nails on a chalkboard.

No. That's not quite right.

Psychological warfare to break the community's will.

Torture.

The Sycamore Slopes and Psychological Suffering. The alliteration pleased him. He forced his full attention onto Hank. "It's about more than the kids. You have skin in this game."

Or ears.

Hank turned away, and Ben followed his gaze out the window.

Shrieks and laughter echoed in the valley as community children played and enjoyed the fresh air. This was the exercise Emma insisted they needed. But at what cost? Was it fair their healthy lifestyle cost Hank his solitude? But it wasn't the kids' fault either. The park had never been this busy until some businesses started setting up these pop-up stores. Now people could stay longer, warm up and fuel up, and head back out to skate and sled some more.

"Is it possible that part of the reason you wrote the letter and started the petition against the slopes was because you've had it with the noise and the rudeness?"

"Wouldn't you?" Hank snapped. He launched himself across the room and disappeared into the front entrance. The click of the door latch, a waft of cold air, and bellowing followed. "Read the sign! It says stay off my property!"

The door slammed so hard the window near Ben rattled in its frame.

A cluster of teens hurried down a track that cut right across Hank's yard.

"I should booby-trap the place. That'll teach those hooligans." Hank slumped into a recliner with more wrinkles than him.

Emma was right. Hank's concern was for his property and peace of mind, not the community. Not that he blamed the man. But small-town grievances made for boring articles. Emma called him a grinch. *The Grinch that Stole Sledding*.

Too harsh. He trashed it.

Hank flipped up the footrest on his chair. He could probably police the front yard and the trail from this vantage point. A steamy mug rested on the stained wood side table. A folded newspaper with the crossword facing up and a large remote control with only four buttons rested beside it. Was this how the man spent his days? Looking for reasons to get angry?

"Lois planted bulbs in that corner." Hank tipped his head in the direction the kids had trekked. He shifted his weight to his left hip and dug knuckle-deep into his pants pocket to retrieve a handkerchief. He dabbed his eyes, wiped his nose, and balled up the fabric, stuffing it back into his pocket when he was done. "If they keep trampling the spot, the flowers might not come back."

That wasn't how perennials worked, but now wasn't the time to correct Hank's understanding of gardening. This wasn't about the flowers. It was rooted deeper than that.

"What was this neighborhood like before the slopes and the pond became so busy?"

The hard lines in Hank's weathered skin eased. An almost-serene expression rose from somewhere deep inside. "When Lois was alive, we'd walk the trail that circled the park every day. We'd see about twenty different birds, depending on the season and the occasional deer. We even picked enough wild raspberries to make a small batch of jam." His eyes glazed over and drifted to a framed picture on the wall.

Hank and Lois.

Lois, with her head tipped back and laughing, and Hank, looking down at her, smiling. A rare candid from an era that favored formal pictures.

"It was simpler."

A shriek cut into the moment, and Ben winced. "Quieter, too. I'd bet."

"Pfft."

"I'm starting to see the problem. Or, maybe I should say, *hear* the problem."

The wordplay pulled a smile from the man. Ben and

Hank both attended Sycamore Hill Community Church. The man was a bit of a grouch, for sure. He liked to be in charge and enjoyed stirring the pot, always taking the opposing point of view and playing devil's advocate. But somewhere, deep inside, beat a soft heart that missed his wife and wanted the flowers she planted to return every spring.

And those desires were valid and, for the most part, being ignored by the town. Maybe there was more to this article than he thought. *Grieving Man Forced to Sacrifice Wife's Memories.*

Ben had caught glimpses of Hank's softer side in the past. It showed up when the older man taught the youngest in their congregation how to make paper airplanes from old bulletins and then held a contest for the kids, measuring the distance flown and acting as the final judge. But a camel could only carry so much on its back before breaking.

Another shriek.

Hank's chest heaved, and he looked away, but not before Ben saw the dampness in his eyes.

"I think I have what I need for the article. Do you mind if I come back or call on you again to follow-up?"

"Do what you want," he said gruffly. "It won't change anything." His attention lingered on Lois's photo. After several quiet minutes, Hank stabbed a button on the remote control, and the television screamed to life.

No one should be forced to live his final days like

this. Ben had his story, but it wasn't the story he'd assumed he'd be writing when he arrived.

After saying goodbye, Ben retraced his path to his car, when a little action down a side road caught his attention.

Some pushing and shoving between boys.

"It's your fault." One of the Desmount boys shoved a smaller kid, who stumbled, but picked himself up again. The bigger one shoved the kid from behind, knocking him back down. The Desmount boys were a tough bunch. This could go south fast.

"Hey," Ben called out as the largest kid lifted his fist and brought it down hard.

Oomph. The boy staggered and dropped to his knees.

Ben broke into a run. "Hey!"

"Lucky for you, your uncle's here!" The oldest brother tossed a snowball at the body curled on the ground.

Uncle? *Nico!*

Ben slid on his knees to Nico's side. "Nico, are you okay?"

Nico rolled onto his back and squinted. "Uncle Ben?"

Ben sagged. No slurred speech. Nico recognized him. What were the other things Emma had checked for?

Nico pushed himself up until he was sitting, keeping a hand over his eye.

"Let me see." Ben pried his hand off. "That's going to leave a mark."

"It'll be fine." Nico shrugged as if it was no big deal. "It's always fine."

Ben stiffened. "Always? This has happened before?"

Nico looked at the brick on the building behind Ben as if it had become the most fascinating piece of art the world had ever known.

"Nico—"

"Only since the talk about shutting down the slopes. It's my fault for getting hurt."

"You know that's not true."

He shrugged again. "No big deal. I can fix this."

Ben frowned. "This isn't something you should have to fix."

Nico avoided meeting Ben's eyes. "I need to get home before Mom wonders where I am."

Claire.

His sister carried enough stress with Matt on deployment. She didn't need this. "After your head injury, a fist to the face isn't something we brush off. You're coming with me to see Emma. I'll call your mom once we know you're okay."

Ben held out a hand and pulled Nico to his feet. Nico swayed a bit, then stabilized. "I can feel my heartbeat in my eye."

"I don't think that's something to be proud of." Ben slung an arm around Nico's shoulder and led him toward his car. They were walking through the clinic doors in less than ten minutes.

Janelle sat in the waiting room with her mother. She gingerly held her left wrist with her right hand.

Ben's gut hardened. Were the boys beating on Janelle, too? It was bad enough that Nico took a hit, but he was bigger. Stronger. The idea of a girl being victimized did something to his insides. It wasn't that girls were weaker. He'd tussled with Emma the night they'd met, and she showed him a thing or two about a woman's power. It was more that they deserved to be protected. It was how God had designed it. Men were to honor women. Not harm them.

"Nico? What happened?" Emma's concern cut through Ben's thoughts. She'd exited the examination room. "You can take Janelle back now," she said to Kellie.

Emma knelt in front of Nico, and with the most tender of touches, she prodded his face, all around the fast-growing bruise. They may be on opposite sides of the debate about the slopes, but they both loved Nico. Would that be enough when his sympathetic article on Hank hit the stands?

Chapter Six

"About how many injuries a year do you see from the slopes and the pond?" Mr. Sycamore slid his reading glasses down his nose and peered at Emma over the top of them. She resisted the urge to squirm. If he was on her side, the side of keeping the slopes open, why were all his questions so prickly?

The town council requested her presence at the meeting tonight, and she was happy to oblige. But she didn't expect to be dropped in the hot seat. Had they been upfront with her regarding the information they sought, she would have pulled files and come prepared with stats. As it was, she could only estimate. "I don't have my charts in front of me, but it is safe to estimate that I see one to two bone injuries, be it bruises or breaks, and several possible concussions each year connected to the slopes or pond."

Mr. Sycamore frowned, and a murmur rippled

through the meeting room in Sycamore Hill Community Church's packed sanctuary. There was no separation between church and state in a town this size. Not when the authorities needed a larger space than usual due to the volume of people who expressed a desire to speak.

"Is this year more than usual, or has that been consistent over the years?" It was Mr. Martin's turn to stare her down, and she could guess where his questions were headed. The man was a shark in the courtroom. Aggressive, sometimes unreasonable, and willing to fight. When convinced of his position, he rarely backed down.

"As the winter activities have increased, so have the incidences requiring my care."

He nodded and made a note.

She, of course, was just telling the truth in answer to a question, but these honest answers were tanking her cause because no one was asking the right questions. Sure, there were more injuries, but it was a proportional increase. "Can I say something?"

Mr. Sycamore and Mr. Martin looked to Pastor Owen, who nodded his approval as the moderator of the town meeting.

"Before the winter activity in town increased, child obesity was on the rise. I frequently saw kids as young as ten struggling with depression that I linked to not getting outside enough. I saw kids with what medical professionals call gaming-posture. It's when the curve in their neck and spine is more pronounced as a result of excessive use of their gaming systems. Bad posture leads to headaches and spine alignment issues. But nobody was concerned about those stats. Nobody called me into a meeting to ask how the town could intervene for the sake of the kids." Emma's attention moved around the room, landing on parents, teachers, and the people she expected to support her argument.

She avoided Ben.

He gathered at the back of the room with a handful of other reporters from nearby newspapers. Grander News had picked up his coverage of the debate splitting the town. Kathryn sat near him, furiously taking notes for her morning show. Emma swallowed the hurt that rose in her throat. *Reporters are neutral.*

"So yes, there have been an increase in injuries since the slopes and the ponds increased in activity, but there has been a decrease in those other conditions. It's my professional opinion that the benefits outweigh the risks."

Ben drew her gaze like a magnet that she was power-less to resist. She tried not to evaluate his reaction to her position, but she couldn't help it. He didn't agree with her. They tip-toed around the issue when they were together, but she followed the coverage, even going as far as to pick up the paper in Grander when they carried the story. She got that Ben couldn't control what assign-ments landed on his desk, but he could control the tone of his articles. He might claim to be neutral—like every journalist did—but he filtered events through his world-view. It was impossible not to. And there was a way to report the truth and still slant it toward a personal bias. She'd seen it in some of his colleagues, but she never thought she'd see it in him.

Her stomach churned. What were the odds that tomorrow's headline would read, *Local Nurse Admits to an Uptick in Injuries*? She pressed a hand to her midsection. After all, they'd been through together, fighting Emergence and cheering for the underdog, she'd thought he was the one person who would always have her back. She hated that she no longer knew for sure where his loyalties lay.

They locked eyes. His chin dipped into his chest, and he pulled his ball cap lower.

A deep and painful breath filled her lungs. She'd lived this debate as a kid and knew what it was to have parents that wouldn't allow her to do anything that came with potential risk. She pretty much spent her childhood with her nose in a book, living vicariously through the characters. Ben's experience differed. One he had yet to share with her fully but was clearly steering his ship. If they couldn't find common ground on something as simple as whether or not children should be allowed to play outdoors, how could they have a future together? Was this God's way of showing her that Ben wasn't the man for her?

"Thank you, Ms. Powles. If no one has further questions for Ms. Powles, we'll move onto the next speaker."

Emma followed Pastor Owen's gaze as it moved down the line of seven people representing Sycamore

Hill's town council. They stretched across the church's stage and included the influential Mr. Martin, Mr. Sycamore, and several other local men and women. When no one objected to her dismissal, he cleared his throat. "Next, we'll hear from the community. Mr. Kovak, you're first."

Emma returned to her seat.

Mr. Kovak approached a microphone standing in the center aisle and briefly rubbed his hands together before pulling off his cap and smoothing his hand over his hair. "Most of you know our family's been having a rough go."

Mrs. Kovak had been into the clinic to see Emma about an issue with her feet. She delivered the mail in town and had been forced into a medical leave while awaiting surgery in the city. The last time Emma had seen her, she'd shared that the financial hit had been hard.

"My wife's off work, and the family ice cream business is struggling. We are barely making ends meet. Who eats ice cream in the dead of winter? But then I opened a pop-up store near the rink and slopes on the weekends, and the hot chocolate and pretzels I sold were enough to make up for the dip in our budget. I'm able to pay my mortgage and even have a bit of a cushion. Closing the slopes will impact my family negatively."

Mr. Sycamore nodded along as Mr. Kovak spoke. Mr. Kovak jammed his hands into his pockets and returned to his seat.

"Please remember to pray for the Kovak family. Mrs.

Kovak's surgery is scheduled for next week," Pastor Owen added. He glanced at the paper in front of him. "Hank Sinclair."

Emma groaned.

Hank strode to the microphone like a man on a mission. "Most of you already know my position. It's been all over the papers."

Emma cut her eyes to Ben again. He pulled his gaze away, but what she saw in it before the shift jolted her heart. Genuine concern. Sympathy. And maybe even a hint of fear. But of what? What could possibly stir fear in him about sledding and skating?

"It's hard to sit at my window and watch reckless kids fly down that hill." Hank jabbed his finger in the direction of a crew of teenagers that filled an entire pew. "Honestly, it's a miracle any of them are still living. It's enough to give an old man a stroke."

A small chuckle rippled through the room.

"Our little dead-end road used to be a quiet place. A happy spot to raise a family. Lois and I had many wonderful years there." His eyes clouded over briefly as if the memory momentarily swept him away. "We chose that spot because it was on the edge of town, yet in town. Farther from the downtown hustle than most neighborhoods. But it feels like downtown has come to us. To me," he corrected. "With all the pop-up businesses—"

"I need that income!" Mr. Kovak shot to his feet.

"And I deserve a little peace and quiet!" Hank retorted.

"Order please," Pastor Owen interjected. "Remember to speak with kindness, even when we disagree."

Especially when we disagree.

"It's Hank's turn to speak. You had your turn."

Mr. Kovak sat back down.

Emma chuckled. A word from Pastor Owen carried more weight than a correction from any town council member, as if the man had a direct line to God's ear. The council knew what it was doing by asking the pastor to moderate.

"Like I was saying, all the little businesses have made parking dangerous. I'm afraid to back out of my own driveway in fear of hitting some kid running ahead of their parents. I just want my neighborhood back."

"Communities change, Hank."

Emma's heart thundered in her chest. She twisted to look behind her. *Ben?*

No, not Ben. It was the guy next to him. Owen gave the press a bit more liberty than the town.

"Neighborhoods change as the needs of the community change."

"At what cost?" Hank's eyes flashed. "What sort of injury does a kid need to get to convince you it's not safe?"

"You can pretend this is about the kids, but we know what it's really about. You're afraid your house value will tank if the park activity grows."

Hank's face turned such a deep shade of red that

Emma tensed, ready to intervene if this became a medical emergency. She gripped the handles of her medical bag. She'd taken to carrying it with her at all times.

"Lay off," Ben cut in gruffly.

Nico's head snapped at the sound of his uncle coming to Hank's defense. The utter betrayal in his eyes broke Emma's heart. Claire wrapped an arm around his shoulder. She leaned in and whispered something into his ear. Nico nodded, and he got up and left.

Ben rubbed the heel of his palm against his chest as if it ached.

"That's enough," Pastor Owen's authoritative command cut through the increasing tension. He didn't have an official place on the town council, but his position as the moderator and his role as the pastor gave him a bit of room. "If we're not careful, this issue will divide the town, the church, and our relationships."

Emma cut her eyes back to Ben and found him already looking at her. Had it already divided them?

"We're better than this," Owen said. "We have to be."

But were they? Meg and Eli Martin, soon to be married, sat on the side of the room that wanted to close the slopes down, probably because Eli's dad had been running numbers and statistics of cases where families sued the town for injuries. Emma had certainly heard enough of that from him.

On the other side of the room, Gloria, Pastor Owen's fiancée, sat with the Sycamores, clearly supportive of keeping the slopes open. She and Pastor Owen were busy planning their wedding, and Emma and Meg had been helping. So far, the tension hadn't seeped into their friendship, but how long could that last?

"The council will take a few days to deliberate, and then we'll announce our decision. For the safety of all concerned, the slopes and the pond will be temporarily closed until we make our decision."

Hank smiled, and the Martin side of the room gave a little cheer.

Who cheers when the children lose?

Emma tapped a loose fist against her heart. At least Nico had left before the devastating announcement. Janelle, sandwiched between her parents, winced. Her hands fluttered like they'd lost track of what they were supposed to be doing. No one appeared to consider how closing the rink would impact the two children the younger population blamed.

Kathryn threaded her way to Emma. "Would you be open to an interview on location? I know you want to keep the slopes open, and I'd like to give you a voice."

"I don't know." Emma rolled her lip into her mouth. Publicly taking a stand against Ben felt wrong. Like she was dishonoring him somehow. But she was allowed to have her own opinion. And he didn't seem to be concerned that his articles opposed her wishes.

Kathryn squeezed Emma's upper arm in a gesture of support. "No pressure. But call me if you change your mind."

The milling crowd swallowed Kathryn and spit out

Ben. He gently moved his gaze over her as if looking for injuries, but emotional wounds didn't present the same way as physical ones. Still, her heart softened at his concern. They might be on opposing sides, but he cared enough to check in. "How are you?"

"Depends. Are you asking for the paper or as my boyfriend?"

Brief hurt flashed across his face, and she immediately regretted her words.

"I'm sorry. I don't know how I feel. It's not what I wanted, and somehow, I feel like my testimony contributed to the outcome."

"You had to be honest. Now, we trust God for the results."

Claire tapped Ben's shoulder from behind. "I'm going to head home. Nico is pretty upset. He's already left. He's sure the kids will all blame him."

Ben's face colored.

"Did you make a decision about Grander News?"

"What decision?" Emma's heart jolted.

"You didn't tell her?" Claire looked at her brother curiously.

Ben rubbed the back of his neck and bit down on his bottom lip. "The newspaper in Grander reached out to me. They might make me a job offer."

"Ah, I gotta go." Claire backed away, her gaze bouncing between them. *Sorry*, she mouthed to her brother.

"The offer you've been waiting for finally came.

Congratulations." An emptiness hollowed her stomach. A million questions pushed to the surface, but she refused to voice any of them. If he had wanted to discuss this with her, she wouldn't have learned about it from his sister. She locked a smile on her face. But her insides swirled.

"I was going to tell you. I was trying to sort it out for myself first." He scraped a hand through his hair, ruffling it.

Emma's fingers twitched to smooth it.

"You might become a big-name reporter yet. It's what you've always wanted. I'm happy for you."

She detached from the moment in the same way she protected herself in medical emergencies. She created emotional distance.

"Emma—" Ben's voice broke.

Those who love greatly risk great hurt. She didn't remember who said it first, but that didn't lessen its truth —this hurt.

Chapter Seven

Ben stuffed his hands into the pockets of his coat and turtled down so the collar covered the lobes of his ears. He avoided eye contact with the people bustling on the street. The shock and disappointment in Emma's expression had burned into his mind. That was not how he had wanted her to find out about his job offer.

He kicked at a chunk of ice in the middle of the sidewalk. He hadn't meant to keep the job offer from Emma. He'd planned to tell her as soon as he figured out how he felt about it. But a day turned into a week, and then he asked Claire for her opinion. And that ring still sat in the box in his bedside table.

Agh. He dragged a gloved hand down his face. He should have told Emma right away. Just like he should tell her about—

His gait hitched. Could he?

How would he start that kind of conversation? *The*

people who were supposed to protect me took my sister and me away from my parents when I was a kid. They had no right.

Ben avoided an icy patch of sidewalk in front of the Muffin Man. He couldn't tell her like that. Detached, as if he were reporting on someone else's life. When he put his history into words, it resurrected the pain, which squeezed his lungs until he could hardly choke out understandable sounds.

Ethan nodded hello as he salted the slick area under his gilded sign. Emma thought Ben's opposition to the slopes flowed from a hard heart instead of a broken and fearful one. She deserved to know the truth. Maybe she'd understand.

My parents did nothing wrong. But the authorities set a chain of events into motion that they couldn't easily reverse.

The door to the Muffin Man opened, and Meg exited the bakery on the arm of Eli. The two lovebirds were only days away from their wedding. Ben and Emma were attending together. Assuming she'd still want to go with him.

"I forgot my textbook." Meg spun on her heel and dashed back inside. Meg's troubled past had followed her to Sycamore Hill, but she and Eli had overcome it.

Lord, if it would help, provide an opening for me to ask them how they did it, how they moved beyond a painful history.

The wind stirred a funnel of loose snow. Eli met

Ben's gaze. "You look like you're carrying a heavy load. Anything I can help you with?"

Shock muddled his thoughts. This was his window. The Lord didn't let any dust settle under his prayer.

Ben swallowed, and a painful lump moved down his throat. "At what point did Meg tell you everything about her past?"

Eli leaned his right shoulder against the red brick exterior of the bakery. The building offered a tiny bit of protection against the wind. "If you mean all the nitty-gritty details, she still hasn't shared it all, and I don't expect her to unless she wants to. But if you mean the general information, the fact she came from abuse, had a daughter that she gave up for adoption, and an ex willing to extort her, she told me in bits and pieces over the first six months we dated."

Ben rolled that over in his mind. He and Emma had been dating longer than six months, and he still hadn't told her. She needed to know.

"Is there something Emma's not telling you?"

"No." Ben shook his head. "It's about me. My past."

Eli nodded. He didn't know the story, so he couldn't comment. Ben's family moved to Sycamore Hill after the *event*. His parents needed a fresh start. They needed a place that didn't know, neighbours who weren't playing out a scene in their mind about what might have happened. They needed people around them that weren't trying to fill in the blanks withheld from the newspaper articles.

Yet, despite those needs, Hank Sinclair knew. Ben's parents confided in the wrong person.

"I'm here for you if you need to talk." Eli's offer pulled Ben back into the present moment.

Meg whooshed out the door, her cheeks rosy and bright and her textbook clutched to her chest.

Ben lifted his chin to acknowledge Eli's offer, and Eli gave a slight nod. They'd chat later. Alone.

If Meg could find acceptance in Sycamore Hill, if her story could be well-received, his would be, too. Ben knew that. But it wasn't just his story to tell. It involved his parents and sister, and they deserved their privacy. Or was that just a convenient excuse? He and Emma weren't married. Not even engaged. His gut heaved. Lame justifications. Especially when the piece of jewelry that would represent her permanent link to him sat in his drawer.

Despite his inability to ascertain his motives, Ben's feet found their way to Emma's clinic. *Lord, help me find the words to share this burden. Prepare her to hear it. Prepare me to tell it in a way that respects and honors the rest of my family.*

He turned up the walkway that led to the clinic's main door as Jackson McGregor jerked his cruiser into the tiny parking lot and jumped from the vehicle. His alert gaze and strong posture, combined with his fast-paced stride, increased Ben's heart palpitations.

Ben broke into a run.

Inside the clinic, Emma stood nose-to-nose with Kellie Holmes. Kellie's gaze moved past Ben, then to

Jackson. When she recognized the officer, she lunged at Emma. "You can't do this!"

Ben dove. It was pure instinct that hurtled him between Kellie and Emma. He latched onto Kellie's arm. If he'd been a few seconds later, she would have struck Emma. Instead, her nails raked down Ben's face. Kellie fought him as Jackson worked quickly to subdue her.

Jackson yanked the woman off Ben, and Ben repositioned himself to keep his body between Emma and Kellie.

"Stop, or I'll cuff you." Jackson's threat bounced off the woman.

"She's my daughter. You can't do this." Kellie thrashed against Jackson. Her bright red complexion and her raw terror touched that place inside Ben that he fought to keep buried.

She looked just like his mom.

And just like that, he was back in time. Back to a day when his mom's eyes grew big, and her lips wobbled. She looked scared, but she was never scared. She squished the spiders in his room and cuddled him after a nightmare. She told Ben everything would be okay when he got sick. But she wasn't saying those words. Whatever the doctor had said, it wasn't okay. It was never going to be okay again.

His mom didn't move toward the police officer. She stepped back, pulling him with her. He stumbled and twisted to look at her face. Fear. Raw terror that he didn't need explained to understand. This wasn't going to have a happy ending. This wasn't going to be a good day.

"Mom?" His voice cracked.

The strange woman knelt to one knee. She held out a hand. "I need you to come with me."

He moved further away. Mom's fingers tightened on his hand. "What's happening?" He looked to the officer. He'd help. He had to. That's what they did.

But he didn't. He said, "Let the boy go. It'll be easier for him if you cooperate."

Let him go? Go where? Ben didn't want to go anywhere. He didn't want to leave his mom. The officer stepped between Mom and him and the strange woman scooped up his hand. He yanked it away. He threw himself at Mom, but the officer caught him.

He reached for her while authorities pulled him away —her clawing the air, trying to touch him. A door closed between them, but it couldn't stop her wailing from assaulting his ears.

"Janelle!" Kellie's screams blended with his mother's.

Ben's eyes found the closed examination room door. Was Janelle hidden back there? Were her hands over her ears? Was she rocking in place, trying to keep back the darkness? Was she crying? Confused? Scared? Was anyone with her?

"My hands were tied." Emma dragged him back into the present scene. That's what the doctor had said to his mother.

Emma's expression paused Ben's inner trauma. There

was no anger or judgment. Just sadness. Profound sadness.

She met and held Jackson's gaze. "The slopes and the rink are closed. When I pressed Janelle for the reason for her new bruises, she froze."

Ben's middle flipped.

"Family and Children services are on their way from Grander."

Jackson led Kellie to a nearby chair. "We need to have a conversation, and escalating things isn't going to help your case."

Janelle peeked out the doorway, tears streaming down her face. "Mom?"

Kellie lunged toward her daughter, and Jackson made good on his previous threat. He pulled out his cuffs and restrained her.

The guilt laced through Janelle's one syllable stabbed Ben right through the heart.

Emma locked her focus on him. "You can't put this in the paper."

"I'd never do that." He choked on the thick words, barely able to force them out.

Emma's white lips and tight features softened. She cautiously approached Janelle. Her posture reminded Ben of how a person might approach a wild animal that needed help but didn't know it. "It'll be okay," she said. "We'll sort everything out. You've done nothing wrong."

She sounded just like the woman with the kind eyes and soft hands who pried him from his mom's arms as she wailed. The keening filled his mind as clearly as if his mom was right here, grieving, pleading, and desperate.

His stomach heaved. Ben lurched toward the nearest trash bin. It took several deep breaths before the feeling of nausea passed. It wasn't twenty-five years ago. It was the present day, and the wails poured from Kellie, not his mom.

"You can't take her away. You can't. Janelle, tell them it was a lie. That you were wrong. Tell them!"

Emma held onto Janelle, who tried to pull out of her arms and run to her mom. "I'm sorry!" Damp lines tracked down her dirty face. She fought against Emma. Her sleeves pulled up, and Ben could see fresh bruising. "It's not true. It's not." Janelle hiccupped and snorted the words.

Bruises were inconclusive. Accidents happened. Injuries didn't equal abuse. Not always. The system didn't always work. It was broken.

He was broken.

He'd sat beside Janelle in the waiting room a few days ago. He chatted with her over the shared fence separating their backyards. How did he miss this? How did he not see? How did the entire town not see it?

He shoved the trash bin away, sank to the floor, and pressed his back against the wall. Was there anything to see? Was it abuse, or was this a horrible repeat of history? He heaved himself up. Wooziness made his head spin. He sat on the nearest chair. He shrank.

Jackson spoke to Kellie, and Emma murmured to

Janelle, who'd twisted herself into Emma's arms. Workers from Children's Aid soon added chaos to the scene, asked questions, and made notes. Jackson led Kellie away, and the workers took Janelle. All the while, Ben sat in the farthest chair, away from the chaos, trapped in a memory.

The officer had handed Ben to the woman, and he'd knocked her glasses off her face. She didn't stop to pick them up. A nurse opened the door, and they whisked him through it.

"MOM!"

He couldn't see her anymore, but he could hear her. Her keening filled the corridor, getting softer and softer as the woman hurried.

"MOM!"

The door flung open, and Mom darted into the hall. She ran toward him, and he reached for her. But before she could reach him, the officer intercepted her. Mom collapsed to the ground, sobbing.

Ben made eye contact with the policeman. His face hardened. It was the first time he ever hated a person.

"Ben?" Emma's palm on his hand jolted him.

How could she do this? How could she take a child from her mother without being sure, one hundred percent sure? A slight defensive shift in her demeanor amplified the questions in his head.

"Ben," she tried again. She stared into his eyes. Probably measuring his pupils.

A shuddering breath shook his body. He'd become a

reporter to right wrongs. To give the mute a voice. To prevent injustice and people in power from overreaching and causing more damage than good. But that world just collided with Emma. The woman he thought he might marry. The woman he had hoped might mother his children had just taken a child from her mother. Emma was the over-reaching power. Emma was the one who ripped a family apart. Emma.

But these weren't Janelle's first bruises. He'd seen them before. He'd seen her. The times she sat on the sidelines, her arm in a sling or a tensor on her wrist, all explained away by a clumsy girl. But if Emma was right, Ben had never seen Janelle. He'd seen what he wanted to see. Janelle was the one in need of a voice, not Kellie. But his mind couldn't handle it. Couldn't comprehend. His body shut down.

"Ben, I need you to look at me." Emma's tone commanded attention.

Her face pinched. It was as if what she saw in his eyes hurt her. But she didn't look away. She searched his expression for assurances that he couldn't give.

"What's going on?" Her question slammed Ben with the force of a tidal wave. He pressed his lips together. If he cracked them even the tiniest bit, vomit would spew everywhere. The bile of his past contaminating his present.

Emma slipped her hands into his and pressed on the webbing between his fingers. The roar in his head lessened. The darkness creeping into his field of vision lightened. His vision cleared. New awareness tightened his senses. Sweat dampened his shirt under his jacket. His cheeks felt wet. Yet Emma didn't pull away. She squeezed his hand, anchoring him to this moment. To her.

"When Claire and I were young," he started, "I got hurt. Nothing serious. Happened on an ice rink."

She held his gaze as if he were the only person in the room.

"My mom monitored it. We had a doctor's appointment the following day, so she didn't take me to the hospital. I was fine."

Emma's hand tightened around his. Did she guess where this headed? Did some part of her intuitively know?

"Our doctor was great. Affirmed that I was likely okay, but referred us to Grander Hospital for some x-rays to make sure." The pressure she put on his hand was the only thing tethering him. If she let go and pulled away, he wasn't sure he'd be able to find his way back. "They thought my mom had abused me."

When it was all over and Ben was back home, they told him he needed counselling. They told him he wasn't okay, and one day his body would force him to deal with the trauma of his past. The body remembered. It always remembered. What wasn't dealt with proactively would be forced to the surface passively.

Nothing about this moment felt passive.

"An unfounded accusation against your parents must have been awful, but this is different. You see that, right?"

Was it?

He felt her breath on his face. "Janelle told me. She told me what has been happening ever since her dad left. Without the easy excuse of the slopes and rink, it all tumbled out of her."

Emma acted on information, not suspicion. But if that was true, why did his insides spin?

Because he still hadn't told Emma the worst. What happened after the accusations. He couldn't. If his mind went there, it might never come back.

Ben inhaled deeply, feeling the expansion in his lungs and holding it. "I know that here." He tapped his temple. "It's just going to take some time to get that here." He patted his chest.

Time, he feared, he didn't have.

Chapter Eight

"I'm so glad you changed your mind." Kathryn grinned widely from where she waited for Emma at the base of the slopes. To the right of Kathryn's booted feet were two over-the-shoulder, waterproof bags, probably to cart her filming equipment around.

Emma rubbed her gloved hands up and down the arms of her puffy jacket. The friction of knitted fabric against the water-resistant shell made a satisfying zipping sound. It distracted her from overthinking. Was her impulsive decision to let Kathryn interview her foolish or wise? After Ben fell apart in her office, her reservations about the slopes and second-guessing her position melted away. His opposing position was not rooted in logic. It was rooted in the trauma of the past. As awful and horrific as that was, the children in the community shouldn't pay the price.

Emma's heart ached for Ben and all he endured, but

it also ached for the local children, whose physical health she was called to care for. Ben had blinders on, falling into "my kingdom come, my will be done" prayers, and his kingdom clashed with what the community needed. The kids needed an adult to step in and say enough was enough. They wouldn't grow into strong adults if they were continually forced to live in a protective bubble.

At least, that was her medical opinion.

Her chest constricted. A tiny prick of guilt stabbed. She wasn't upset Ben's prayers seem to clash with God's will. She was upset his prayers clashed with *her* will.

The snow fell steadily, adding a fresh layer nearly three inches deep to the previous accumulation. Several flakes clung to Kathryn's eyelashes before melting. She wore those fake lashes when filming. They looked great on television, but they were wildly distracting up close. "Have you been waiting long?"

Kathryn shook her head. "I've been here for about an hour filming B roll for the show. I was at the pond for a bit first."

An hour? The sun had only been up that long. Emma couldn't imagine the time of day that Kathryn rose to prepare her face and hair for her morning show. The next time a middle-of-the-night emergency tempted Emma to complain, she'd count her blessings those came infrequently. Kathryn did this every day.

Yellow caution tape blocked the area to the slopes, and another string prevented access to the pond. Would they get into trouble for crossing the line? It wasn't like they were contaminating a crime scene or anything.

"What changed your mind?" Kathryn removed a smaller camera from her bag and slung it over her shoulder. She tilted her head to the left to indicate Emma should follow her.

A million things impacted her decision to meet Kathryn. But mostly, Ben's confession about the authorities investigating his parents for abuse tipped the last domino. But she couldn't say that. She'd never say that. It wasn't her story to tell. He vowed that he'd never let a corrupt authority abuse another kid, but he was too close to see that was happening right now. Not in the same way he faced it as a child, but still valid—still an overreach. A higher power was stealing their childhood.

"I want to help the kids have access to healthy, outdoor fun." Emma skirted around the real motivation. Calling out the leaders in the community for overstepping their bounds and making an arbitrary decision that the children had to pay for would only make matters worse. She only hoped that Ben would understand why she'd done this when he saw the morning show. Why she spoke out publicly.

And she hoped their relationship would be able to withstand the tension.

"And you think the slopes and pond are the best way for kids to maintain a healthy lifestyle?"

"Without outdoor options, they're forced to an indoor alternative. It's not reasonable to expect kids to pack away the remotes when the sun comes out after playing on electronics all winter. They'll be conditioned to favor electronic play by then."

When Ben's head was clear, he'd see they'd always been on the same side. The side that wanted what was best for the kids. He had to.

"Say that again," Kathryn lifted her camera. "Just like that."

Emma was just warming up. "And what's next? Close the pond to swimming because someone might dive into the shallow area? Outlaw bicycles because a child could fall and break a limb? Life is not safe. We can't raise the next generation in a bubble and expect strong children to emerge."

Kathryn's grin widened with each sentence. She pulled her camera back, rewound the film and viewed it. "I got it. Passionate. Outraged. Perfect."

Kathryn lifted the camera again and motioned for Emma to continue.

Emma stiffened. Passionate? Sure. But outraged? Was there ever a place for outrage? Was believing righteous anger filled her a sign of wisdom or pride? Her morning Bible reading plan had taken her to the book of James. What was it that James wrote? You quarrel because you want what you don't have, or something like that. The real root of dispute was selfish desires.

Had her desire for a good thing grown larger than her desire for God's glory and eternal purposes? Had her good desires turned into evil desires? Every person was just a decision away from allowing desire to push them over the edge.

But it wasn't selfish. It was for the kids. Her heart wanted this for the kids. That's why she was fighting for it. That's why it mattered. She pushed her hesitations aside. Her desires had not become sinfully exalted. The fact she was willing to go to war with the town didn't mean she was wrong.

"I have an idea." The thought had hardly formed in her mind before she presented it. The slope in the background beckoned her. "I'll go down the hill and show everyone that if I can toboggan at my age, then there is no need to fear the kids sledding."

Kathryn laughed. The camera shook in her hands. "Love it. Action shots are the money shots. I left a plastic carpet for you at the top of the hill." Kathryn pulled her face out from behind the camera and winked. "Great minds think alike."

Emma hiked up the gentle incline. By the one-quarter mark, her insides had heated enough that there was a distinct difference between the temperature of her booted feet submerged in the fresh snow and her screaming thighs. This aerobic exercise was what the kids needed. She slapped her thighs as they burned. The frosty air coated her lungs. Less screen time and more fresh air.

It felt good. Healthy.

The toe of her boot caught something, and Emma stumbled. She landed on her hands and knees with an oomph. The snow shot up around her and reached her elbows. Her fingers tingled. The thin, knitted gloves were not enough protection from the elements. Emma pushed herself up with a laugh and brushed the snow away, revealing a small rock.

She glanced over at the run the kids took down the slope. No footprints or animal tracks. The steady snowfall made sure of that. But it also meant she couldn't see what was underneath. Her stomach hopscotched. The kids raced down this hill all the time.

When she reached the peak, her breath came faster and puffed in front of her face in clouds of white exhalation. She fisted her hands on her hips and looked down. Not a single mark marred the covering of white.

Though your sins are like scarlet, they shall be as white as snow.

A clean covering to erase a lifetime of stain.

Kathryn gave her a thumbs up from the base. Just behind Kathryn, the rays of early morning light cast hues of gold, pink, and orange over the glistening ice topping the pond. It momentarily took Emma's breath away.

The heavens declare the glory of God, and the sky above proclaims his handiwork.

The wind caught the tips of the trees, and they swayed. Their heavy, snow-laden tops rocked like a church choir.

Then shall all the trees of the forest sing for joy before the Lord, for he comes, for he comes to judge the earth.

What would the Lord find if He came today to judge

Sycamore Hill? Would he be pleased? Would they be found like a bride eagerly awaiting her groom?

"You ready?" Kathryn shouted.

Emma found the plastic carpet wedged between two trees, exactly where Kathryn had said it would be. She rolled it out and positioned herself at the top of the slope. She gave Kathryn a thumbs up. Her stomach flipped again. It looked steeper from this position, and she wasn't as young as she used to be. She inhaled through her nose. *Lord, this is for the kids.*

She pushed off.

For several glorious seconds, she flew down the hill. The wind stung her cheeks. Her hair billowed out behind her. She couldn't help it. A shriek of joy ripped from her body at a volume that probably woke the entire neighborhood. The speed. The wildness. The freedom.

She saw it too late. She yanked left, but momentum wouldn't allow her to change the trajectory. The seemingly innocent tip of a stone poked through the upper crust of the snow. Her mouth twisted in horror.

In reality, it happened in seconds. Milliseconds. But in her body and mind, it slowed down. It moved excruciatingly slowly. Painfully inching through time as her shriek turned from joy to panic. Her body twisted away from the impact. She pinched her eyes, instinctively protecting her core as the rock broke her descent.

The next thing Emma knew, she was on her side, cradling her arm, writhing. Her arm burned. White-hot stars seared her eyes. Nausea tore through her midsection. She turned her head to the side and vomited. Every movement sent molten pain coursing through her.

Kathryn's face hovered over her. "Don't move. I've already called for help."

Emma opened her eyes and tried to speak, but a jarring blast of lightning stole her words. She pinched her eyes closed. She nodded. It sent another wave through her.

Shock. She must be in shock.

She wanted Kathryn to put a blanket or something around her, but then she realized Kathryn already had.

Good.

Her right hand cradled her left arm. She tried to move, and white clouded her eyes. Nope. Not doing that again.

"I've got you."

Ben. How did he get here so fast?

The warmth of his voice took the edge off the chill deep in her bones. Ben would take care of her. Ben would make sure she was okay. Ben loved her. He wouldn't let anything bad happen to her.

She felt hands probing her body. She caught a few words like stick. Splint. Careful. Followed by the sensation that someone was preparing to lift her and the realization that this would hurt.

Brightness exploded behind her eyelids. Then, it all went dark.

. . .

Emma roused to the rocking of a vehicle. The hum of an engine vibrated in her head. But she was no longer cold. That was nice.

Voices mixed. Sounds, not words. Urgent.

Darkness again.

Then lights. Bright, blinding lights that she could see even though her eyes were closed.

"It's Emma." A voice shook.

She should know that voice. She tried to open her eyes, but a stickiness held them together. Despite extraordinary effort, she couldn't let in a sliver of light.

"You'll be okay, Emma," the same voice assured her.

She felt the softness of a mattress under her and lost track of the words trying to sort themselves into an understandable format.

Where was Ben? Was he here?

Emma moaned. Something poked through her skin, and warmth crawled up her arm. It spread through her middle with increasingly thickening tentacles and inched down to her toes. A weight compressed her body. She nearly sighed with relief.

Like a weighted blanket. She didn't have a weighted blanket.

She must be at the hospital.

Her brain strained, connecting fuzzy dots. Medicine. They must have given her med—

Her head rolled to the side. Someone turned the volume down. They dimmed the lights.

Everything went black.

Chapter Nine

Ben couldn't slow the panic galloping through his chest despite the nurses assuring that Emma was okay, and it was normal for her to still be out from the pain medication. Even with massive doses, her features occasionally tightened. Her eyes pinched. Her head rolled to the side. Small moans escaped. Emma hadn't opened her eyes in a long time. She looked so fragile.

Had his pigheadedness caused this? Why had he been so consumed with getting his way? He should have led her to love and enjoy God more deeply, not pushed her to impulsive decisions. The boa constrictor around his gut tightened further.

Anger sparred with guilt. His blood heated, the emotions as equally strong as his love. What had she been thinking?

"Is she awake yet?" Kathryn set a to-go coffee cup on the wheeled tray that Ben pushed up against the wall.

"No."

"How was her night?"

"Painful, but the nurses insist that's normal, which is good. I guess." He dragged a hand down his face. The stubble on his jaw scratched his palm. "They think she should wake up soon."

Kathryn's gaze lingered on Emma's face. "I guess this is it for the slopes, then. You win."

Out of all the words Ben could use to describe what had transpired, win wasn't one of them. As much as he wanted to keep the kids and Nico safe, sadness darkened the victory. This wasn't what he wanted. Not by a long shot.

"Hank will exploit the accident to prove the slopes should be banned for good." Her gaze never left Emma's face.

Hank. Ben slumped in his chair.

The man arrived on the scene almost as quickly as Ben. He'd been so distraught. Ben had briefly wondered if he'd require medical attention. Maybe he cared more about the community than they had given him credit for.

Kathryn pulled a chair to the other side of the bed. "Something about the way Emma fell seemed off to me."

Her thoughtful expression piqued his interest. "What do you mean?"

"I can't put my finger on it. I've watched the video—"

Ben straightened. "You have video footage?"

"I was recording for the morning show."

"Can I see it?"

Kathryn pulled out her phone. "It automatically syncs with the cloud, so I can access it anywhere." She scrolled through the selection. "Here it is." She handed the phone to Ben.

Emma trudged up the slope, slowing a bit as the incline steepened. She looked so full of life. Full of joy. How had they let things escalate to the point of hospitalization? In the video, Emma's sincerity shone. She cheerfully served her community using her gift and abilities on the platform God had given her. Her expression held none of the contempt that filled Hank's face when Ben interviewed him.

When Emma reached the top, she stopped to appreciate the view. Was she thinking of the Lord and His glorious handiwork? She plucked a sled from between two trees and positioned herself on the plastic carpet.

An internal snake constricted his intestines. His lips tingled, knowing what was coming.

Emma pushed off.

Kathryn had zoomed in, and she followed Emma's descent with a steady hand. Midway down the hill, Emma launched into the air before her body crumpled into a heap. Even in the video, he could tell from how her body automatically accommodated her clavicle that the injury was severe.

His stomach rolled, but he slid the video back until right before the launch and watched it again.

And again.

And again.

Something was off.

"What do you see?" Kathryn lifted her chin.

"I'm not sure. Something seems—"

Emma moaned.

Ben hurriedly handed the phone back to Kathryn and scooped up Emma's good hand. "Emma? Are you awake? Open your eyes, Emma."

Her head lolled to the side.

Kathryn hurried into the hall, calling for a nurse.

"Come on, Emma. You can do it. Open your eyes." An iron fist clutched his lungs. He couldn't breathe. Not until she opened her eyes.

She blinked.

Relief uncoiled his stomach. "That's my girl." Ben tenderly pushed her hair off her forehead. Why did it take an accident to realize how much he loved her? Why was that blasted ring still in his bedside table? It should be on her finger, declaring his undying love.

He'd strayed. He'd become consumed by fear and what-ifs. But the soul consumed with God was less easily offended. That's who he wanted to be. Who Emma needed him to be—consumed with God.

She turned toward his voice, and his insides leaped.

"Do you feel pain?"

Emma's tongue poked out and bumped along her lips. "Water?"

Ben lifted a cup of water and put the straw in Emma's mouth. "Take a sip."

"Thank you." Her eyes drifted closed again.

"Do you remember what happened?"

She rolled her lips for a second. Before she could answer, a nurse bustled in with Kathryn on her heels.

"Emma, it's good to see you awake." The nurse checked Emma's vitals and made a note on her chart. "Are you in much pain? What number are you on the pain scale?"

"Seven." Her eyes stayed shut.

"I'll see what I can do for that. You've broken your clavicle."

Emma's eyes popped open. The whites glowed brightly at the nurse's words. Did she forget what happened? She sought Ben, and he leaned forward so she could easily see him. "I'm here."

The panic in her gaze lessened.

"You broke it when you fell off the sled."

"It's a non-displaced fracture," the nurse said. "An X-ray showed no movement."

The panic in Emma's eyes lifted.

"That means the bone is broken, but it remained in place," the nurse explained for Ben's benefit. "I'll see if I can find the doctor. He'll want to know that you're awake." The nurse hurried off.

Emma's gaze stuck to Ben. "What happened?"

He didn't like Emma's confusion. She should remember. She didn't hit her head. At least, he didn't think she hit her head. The angle of the video didn't provide a definitive answer.

"What do you remember?" Ben carefully touched Emma's hand, so he didn't disturb the IV line.

She squeezed her eyes shut. "I remember walking to the top of the hill." Her lids popped open. "I was sledding. Kathryn was there."

"She's still here." Ben gave a shaky laugh.

"Hi, Emma." Kathryn leaned into Emma's field of vision.

She turned toward Kathryn's voice. "Sorry to ruin your morning show."

"Don't worry about that. You just focus on getting better." Kathryn made it sound like no big deal that her show ran a repeat, but Ben knew better; Kathryn didn't run repeats. He loved that she prioritized her friend over her career.

"What else do you remember?" Ben prodded.

Emma pulled her lower lip into her mouth. Ben hated the tiny indicators of pain in the corners of her eyes. Whatever meds they were giving her, they weren't enough.

Her eyes opened fully. "The sled hit something. Something hard."

That would explain the odd angle that Emma shot into the air. She had sledded down the middle of the slopes. It was the same run the kids had used hundreds of times. If something had been buried there, it would have been discovered by now. "We noticed something was off in the video."

Kathryn stood up and slipped her arms into her

jacket. She slung her purse strap over her shoulder. "There shouldn't be anything under the snow on the hill. I've recorded video several times. I'm heading back to take a look around. I want to see if I can find whatever it was that Emma hit."

Emma lifted her good hand to Kathryn. "Don't let anyone else go down."

Kathryn's features softened, and she squeezed Emma's fingers. "You don't have to worry about that. Hank saw the accident, and he's taken it upon himself to sit outside at the base of the slopes and ensure no one uses it."

Emma turned her face away, but not before Ben noted her sadness. He caught Kathryn's eye. "Let me know what you find?"

She nodded. Kathryn leaned over the bed and looked tenderly at her friend. "I'll call you later, okay?"

The corners of Emma's lips turned up slightly.

Kathryn passed the doctor as she exited.

"It's good to see you awake, Emma."

"Hi, Dr. Blake."

"You were pretty banged up. Maybe you should leave the sledding to the kids. Their bones are more forgiving."

She chuckled, then winced.

The doctor explained her injury and treatment with medical jargon that Ben didn't quite follow, but Emma tracked, which dissolved any lingering fears she might have suffered from a head injury.

"You've passed the twenty-four-hour mark, and you're doing well. We'll likely discharge you later today."

"Today?" Ben massaged the back of his neck. That seemed a bit fast.

Dr. Blake flicked his gaze to Ben briefly. "Yes. She'll heal quite well with conservative management. She runs no risk of damaging the blood vessels, since bone fragments were not created. All she needs now is pain management and rest." He turned back to Emma. "How's the clinic going?"

Right. Emma would know the doctor. She worked at this hospital before opening the clinic in Sycamore Hill.

The mention of the clinic made Emma try to push herself upright, but her face pinched, and she let herself down gently. Ben held up an extra pillow, and Emma nodded. She supported her arm that was in a sling as he slipped an extra pillow behind her. "What does Emma's injury mean for the clinic?"

Dr. Blake sighed deeply. The sound made Ben's heart lurch.

"You'll have to temporarily shut down."

Emma's eyes filled with tears. The clinic meant everything to her. "What about my patients?"

"They'll have to come here like they did before the clinic opened."

Emma took in a sharp breath. She blinked quickly.

Ben would give anything to take the disappointment from Emma. If he could go back in time, he'd—

Well, he didn't know what he'd do. They still fundamentally disagreed on what was best for the community. But at the very least, he'd stop her from going down that hill.

"I know this is disappointing, Emma. But it won't be for long. Just until you are off the strongest of the pain medications. Maybe a week, then you'll be able to manage with acetaminophen or ibuprofen." Ben appreciated the way Dr. Blake gave Emma his full attention. He wasn't taking notes or itching to move on to the next patient. He gave every appearance of having all the time in the world.

"What if I refused to take the meds? Could I work then?"

She'd do that? Ben started to object, but Dr. Blake cut in. "You still wouldn't be able to practice. Without the meds, the pain would prohibit you from working. I'm sorry."

A single tear slipped down her cheek.

The doctor patted the bedsheets. "I know, it's disappointing, but the clinic will still be there when you've recovered. You need time to heal, and that's not going to happen if you're moving your arm, neck, and head. Just stay still. Rest." He glanced at Ben. "Are you staying for a while?"

They'd have to drag him away.

Ben nodded.

"I'll check in again later. And I mean it. Try to get some rest."

"What's the total recovery time?" Ben asked before Dr. Blake could leave.

"Two to three months."

"Months?" Ben blurted.

"Our bodies are amazing things, but healing from something like this takes time. There is no way to speed the process of a bone knitting itself back together."

The silence that followed Dr. Blake's departure lay heavier than one of the hospital's weighted blankets. "I'm sorry, Emma."

"I was trying to prove the slopes were harmless fun. Instead, I made the opposition's case." She blew out her cheeks. "You're welcome."

His stomach plummeted. She lumped him in with the opposition? Sure, things had been tense between them since they'd landed on opposing sides of the debate, but she had to know that he was always for her. He wanted good things for her. "This isn't what I wanted."

She focused on the wall behind his right shoulder. She looked past him. Not at him.

"Emma?" His voice cracked. He leaned his weight onto the edge of the mattress. She couldn't believe he'd be happy with this. None of this is what he wanted.

What did he want?

Yesterday, he might have said he wanted the slopes closed and a guarantee that everyone he loved would be safe. That was what he'd been fighting for, but he'd reaped the opposite. Today, he wanted Emma to be healthy. He wanted to give her back her clinic. He wanted the debate about the slopes to be settled, and it surprised him to realize he didn't care how the vote swayed anymore. Today, he wanted whatever would make Emma happy.

She looked at him. Finally. His heart sank. She still saw him as the enemy. His phone vibrated in his pocket.

Emma turned away. "Are you going to get that?"

He withdrew his phone, fully intending to silence it until he saw the display. "It's Claire. Someone must have told her what happened."

He tapped the speaker icon on the phone. Before he could assure Claire that Emma was okay, Claire blurted, "Nico's missing."

Chapter Ten

Emma gritted her teeth as she carefully folded herself into Ben's vehicle. Hot waves rolled through her, muddying her mind even with the pain meds. She forced her expression to stay neutral and relaxed, but inside, she slogged through sludge. If Ben caught even a whiff of her fog, he'd force her to stay in the hospital. But she'd checked out earlier than planned because Nico needed her.

The car rocked as Ben slammed her door closed, and she clamped her teeth against an ambush of pain. Emma fumbled one-handedly with the seatbelt to cover her discomfort. The sling and swathe setup restricted her gross movement. She was right-handed and could grab the strap and stretch it over her body, but she couldn't click the latch plate into the buckle.

The tightness in her chest advanced to her neck, shrinking her windpipe and bleeding into jaw pain.

Burning increased the ache in her injuries. She bit back a scream. *She was useless*! It would be weeks before she could lift or shift her affected arm. Months before she was back to normal. She ground her teeth together, and the ache in her jaw crept to her ear.

Ben connected his phone to Bluetooth and got his sister back on the line before helping Emma with her seatbelt and clicking his own. His movements were simple, seamless, and second nature. She couldn't even fasten her seatbelt.

"What's happening?" Ben barked as soon as Claire picked up the call.

"The school phoned. Nico never showed today."

Ben's jaw moved back and forth. A muscle near the hinge twitched. Emma braced herself against the lunge of the vehicle as Ben thrust it into gear and tore out of the parking spot. The clock on the dash changed by one minute, and Emma started counting that twitch in his jaw. When she'd reached one hundred and twenty before the minute number changed again, she stopped counting and began to pray.

"Are the Desmount boys at school?"

The cell connection crackled. "I don't know. Why?"

The car lurched at the lot's pay station. Ben swiped his credit card to pay for parking, and the vehicle jerked again. Sharpness exploded in her shoulder. She bit back a cry, turning her face toward the window. Weight pushed against her eyes and sinuses. The meds should kick in at any moment. She just needed to hold on until then.

"I caught them giving Nico a hard time." Ben's ejected words seeped through his clenched teeth.

"When?" Claire's voice sharpened.

Nico had failed to tell his mom about the shouting match on the street that led to his black eye. Emma snorted. Of course, Nico didn't tell his mom. He wouldn't have said anything to Ben except Ben stumbled upon the fight in progress. Every kid that graced her clinic abided by some unspoken honor code that refused to snitch.

"A few days ago." The sharp lines of Ben's jaw dominated his features despite the scruff filling his neck and cheeks. There was something primal about him all unshaven, natural, and intense. He was ready to stand in the gap and fight for his family.

An odd noise gurgled from his throat. Ben was a fighter, but could he manage this? Could he manage when the hits landed this close to home?

"What can we do, Claire?" Emma cut in.

"Emma? What are you doing out of the hospital?"

"They released me."

"You left against the doctor's orders," Ben cut in. "He was going to release you later tonight."

"You didn't need to do that," Claire's words thickened.

"Yes, I did." Emma's reply nearly stuck in her swollen throat. Ben may not have put a ring on her finger, but she loved Claire like a sister and Nico like a nephew. She'd face an invading army for them.

Claire's shuddering breath said enough.

Ben's gaze hijacked Emma's attention. It hung on her face, assessing her pain. "Why don't I drop Emma with you? Then I'll go help search."

"Sounds good."

They disconnected.

"What were the Desmount boys beating on Nico for?" Emma hoped her grimace might be interpreted as concern. She screwed her lips to the left and compressed them.

"They blamed him for the slopes being closed."

Emma reached her good hand across her body and over the center console. She gently touched Ben's leg. "It's not your fault. You don't even know if it's connected."

His lips twitched as if he was trying to find the right words. "I pushed so hard. I thought I knew what was best. I thought I could protect him." His voice cracked.

"We can't protect the people we love from life."

He flinched. "No, but we should be able to protect kids from harm." Ben scrubbed a hand down his face and shook his head like he needed to clear it.

"Tell me more about the Desmount boys." The pain medication Dr. Blake administered ambushed her faculties like a burst dam. Emma sighed at the rush of relief. She channeled her energy into sharpening her thoughts. Agony faded to a dull throb, but relief made everything fuzz around the edges.

"Nico kept muttering something about fixing it."

"Fixing it." She let her lids close and rolled the phrase in her mind. "If you were a kid, how would you fix a closed sledding hill?"

Her eyes snapped open. They spoke simultaneously. "Find a new one."

Ben's Adam's apple bobbed. "This is good." He poked his tongue into his cheek.

"Where else can kids toboggan?" Her muddied thoughts refused to cooperate.

"Grander. But if Nico was trying to appease class-mates, he'd stay local." Ben drummed the pads of his fingertips on the steering wheel.

"We don't have other hills."

"Are there short runs that lead into drainage ditches?"

The hair on her nape and arms lifted. Nico was smarter than that. He had to be. "He'd want something equal or better than the old hill. That would be the only way to stop the bullying."

They fell silent. Ben changed lanes to pass a Grander City garbage truck headed toward Sycamore Hill.

"Grander City brings its garbage to a Sycamore Hill landfill, right?" Emma asked.

"They have been using our landfill for a while now. It's how Sycamore got the funds to revamp parts of the downtown."

"And we had a fresh snowfall, right?" Emma fought hard against wooziness.

"That would transform a mountain of garbage into a

pristine sledding hill." Ben shook his hand and waved her suggestion off. "But the landfill isn't open to the public. It's not like he can waltz in there and start playing around and have nobody notice."

Sure, she didn't know Nico like Ben, but she knew boys. And she never met a boy that a chain-link fence could stop.

Ben changed lanes again. A car horn blared behind them as Ben cut across the highway and took the exit ramp.

Emma's mouth dried up. She supported her aching arm as the momentum pressed her body against the sling, pain working almost as well as adrenaline to revive her. "Where are you going?"

"There's one more man-made hill we haven't considered."

Every location in town scrolled through her mind, and she discarded each one as it popped up. Ben's gaze slammed into hers as if he just realized how his impulsive driving might impact her body. "How's the pain?"

Higher than it should be, but she'd never tell him that. Never. The only thing that mattered was finding Nico before he got hurt. She ground her teeth. "I'll be fine."

They neared the historic residential area of Sycamore Hill, and Ben slowed the vehicle until they inched along.

Understanding dawned. The construction site!

"Maybe I'm crazy, but when Nico and I were here, he

commented on the hill the excavator created. It was twice the size of the slope."

And it was only protected by that flimsy orange construction fencing. "The angle of that hill—" Her voice cracked. There was no way Nico tobogganed down that hill without sustaining an injury. There wasn't enough space at the bottom. He'd collide into whatever equipment stood there, shoot out into the street, or— She forced herself to stop. Catastrophizing wasn't going to help.

Just seconds ago, Emma had scoffed at the idea of a fence being a strong enough barrier to stop a boy. Now, she desperately needed to believe it could hold back Nico's determination.

Ben's knuckles whitened as he gripped the steering wheel.

Lord, please, keep Nico safe. They wove through the streets of Sycamore Hill. *Have mercy, God. Please.*

Ben parked the car across from the building site. Bright orange temporary fencing wrapped the entire block. "You stay here. I'll take a quick look."

Emma's imagination raced. There were a million places and ways Nico could be hurt. If she was seriously wounded from a rock under the snow on a slope with a reasonably gentle descent, how much worse could it be for Nico on a hill angled to launch him like a rocket?

Ben disappeared around the corner.

Lord, please. Emma scanned the area in the opposite direction, looking for any hint of the boy. Her breath hitched in her throat. A backhoe, wooden pallets, lumber with a tarp covering it.

Where was he? Were they wasting time? Nico didn't have time. This made sense. It was the only logical place for him to go. But boys were not always rational.

Front-load tractor. A skid steer. A forklift. All powered down, waiting for the finances to start up again.

Blue. Bright blue. She backtracked. One ice-cold moment of incomprehension and then she knew—the same blue as Nico's jacket.

Amongst the piles of lumber was an out-of-place blue lump. A burst of clarity revived her mind. Adrenaline-induced hyper-alertness only lasted a few minutes, so she moved quickly. She pressed the button to release her seatbelt, and it retracted automatically. Cold air blasted her face as she pushed open the car door, and as carefully as possible, so as not to bump her injury, she exited. Every step shot fresh agony through her gut. She glanced in the direction Ben had gone. He'd come around the other side soon enough once he circled the block. She started toward the lump of blue.

The closer she got, the more her heart hammered in her chest. Her stomach somersaulted when she spied the hole cut into the mesh fencing.

At the bottom of a dirt pile capped with snow lay a body.

"Ben!" Time slipped sideways.

Emma's slow progress forward shot stabbing pain through her body. She fought a wave of light-headedness as she contorted her body to fit through the broken fencing. *She was not passing out. She was not passing out.* Sweat beaded on her forehead.

The footsteps pounding behind her increased, but she kept her eyes forward. Nico. She had to get to Nico.

Lord, help. Help me help Nico. Clear my thoughts. Make me able. She steeled herself. In her peripheral vision, she registered Ben surpassing her, hurdling a pallet, and dropping to his knees. Her scream brought the residents out of their homes. Someone had to have called an ambulance already.

She limped, her gait slowed by pain.

Finally.

There.

At the sight of his white, still face, another dose of adrenaline rocketed through her.

Nico's chest rose and fell.

"His airway is clear, and he's breathing." Emma carefully lowered herself to her knees and swallowed bile threatening to escape her throat. She turned and gagged, only to have nausea amplified by the pharyngeal reflex. It was like a twisted merry-go-round with no place to get off and find her bearings.

She pressed the fingertips of her good hand to Nico's wrist. "Pulse is good."

Every movement sent hot streaks through her body. She couldn't pass out.

Nico's eyes fluttered. "Uncle Ben?"

Emma leaned in. "Nico, what hurts?"

"My head." His eyes drifted closed again, then his body convulsed.

"Roll him onto his side." Emma fumbled the automatic response to adjust Nico's positioning, and the pain crumpled her.

Ben supported Nico, but his eyes latched on hers. "Are you okay?"

She ground her molars and fought fresh waves of nausea. One curt nod was all Ben needed to refocus on Nico.

Lord, help.

Ben held Nico on his side, eyes continually darting from her to Nico. The last she needed was to be a distraction.

"I'm fine," she barked. "Focus on him."

But she wasn't fine. She wasn't even close to fine.

Chapter Eleven

The paramedics loaded Nico into the back of the ambulance. His body filled three-quarters of the adult-sized stretcher, and his pale skin faded even more against the white sheets.

"We'll follow in the car." Ben squeezed his sister's shoulder. Ben had been on the phone with Claire when Emma had screamed. He'd shouted his location and disconnected. Claire arrived on the scene before the paramedics. The medics had to come from Grander city.

Claire climbed into the back of the ambulance and perched beside Nico. The weariness carved into her expression sent currents of guilt ripping through Ben. All he wanted was to keep Nico safe. But Ben brought him to the building site that day he'd interviewed Franklin Cooper. Ben might as well have shoved the boy off the peak of dirt himself.

Emma stepped shoulder to shoulder with Ben,

cradling her arm. A warm sensation expanded his chest. She'd pushed through her pain, denying it at every turn, prioritizing Nico. She was the hero of this story.

Before Ben could comment on the darkening circles under her eyes or her pained, watery gaze, a medic joined them. His brows furrowed, and his lips pursed as he carefully looked Emma up and down. Slowly. In a way that indicated they knew each other. That inner warmth in Ben's chest started to burn. He shifted closer to Emma, so they were viewed as together, not merely standing side by side.

"Are you okay?" The medic's question was appropriate considering the circumstances, but it came across as personal—even familiar.

"I will be," Emma deflected. She tossed a sidelong glance Ben's way. Pinched features contradicted her words.

"I'll take her to the hospital, Ryan." Ben read the name stitched onto the medic's uniform. "I'll make sure she gets looked at again."

Ryan scrutinized Ben, and Ben lifted his chin. A powerful urge to be found sufficient rushed through his veins. Ryan jutted his chin in Emma's direction. "Don't let her bully you into believing she's okay when she's not."

Yeah, the man knew Emma, all right. Ben couldn't help but smile, but the second his features shifted into one, guilt landed like an anvil. How could he smile while an ambulance carted away his nephew and while Emma was battered and bruised?

A second paramedic that had been busily hooking Nico up to all sorts of machines called out the open bay doors. "Ready."

Ben sought Claire. "He'll be okay," he promised. That wasn't a promise within Ben's power to keep. He knew it, and she knew it, but he said it anyway because he had to believe it was true.

Lord, please.

Claire curled over Nico's body, her face close to her son's as she whispered to him. She carried so much weight, usually with an appearance of ease, always with grace. Her husband was deployed more than he was home. She didn't need this crisis. Not on her home turf. Not where she was supposed to feel safe and secure.

Not when Ben was supposed to carry the weight for her.

A boulder of guilt snowballed larger and larger as it rolled downhill. He'd failed to recognize Janelle needed help. He'd failed Nico. He'd failed Claire. He failed. The two words repeated in his mind over and over until they were all he heard.

After a quiet word with Emma, Ryan closed the ambulance's bay doors and slipped into the front. It pulled onto the street. No siren. No lights. That was a good sign. It had to be. Neighbours that had emerged from the chaos and noise slowly made their way back into their homes.

Ben slipped his arm around Emma's waist loosely, careful not to touch any part of the sling and swathe. She slumped into his side. Her head turned, and she rested her cheek on his shoulder. Her entire body shuddered. The strength she'd projected since they'd found Nico drained. He pressed a kiss against the top of her sweaty head. At some point, she'd lost her hat. He aided her back to his car.

The ginger way she compensated for the left side of her body, combined with her lack of conversation, told him all he needed to know. He didn't push her. She'd pushed herself far enough already. She didn't complain, but pain laced every step, movement, and expression. She could say she was okay as much as she wanted, but she wasn't.

Still, she did what she had to do. The adrenaline carried her, but the crash was imminent. After Emma had briefed the paramedics and released Nico to their care, it was as if someone had pulled the plug on her energy.

All because she loved Nico more than she cared about her recovery.

He helped Emma settle in the front seat and latched her seatbelt. They headed back in the direction they'd come. She still hadn't said anything beyond a simple *thank you* and *yes, please* to his offer to help. Her silence afforded him time. Too much. How did they end up here? How did a ridiculous sledding hill lead them to this spot, with Emma post-surgery and Nico in an ambulance? Ben scrubbed a hand down his face. His whiskers scraped his palms.

"I'll be okay." Her words came out rougher than his bristled chin.

He ground his teeth. She should be saving energy, not wasting it on a pep talk.

"Nico has seen the growing dirt pile every day, just like the rest of us."

A vein along his jaw started to throb. But Ben was the one who'd taken him there. Ben was the one who'd brought Nico with him to hear that Franklin Cooper had paused the build indefinitely, which meant there was no one on the grounds. Ben was the one that championed the closing of the old hill and practically pushed Nico toward this one.

But he couldn't say that. Saying it out loud would make it true, and he couldn't let it be true. He wanted to protect the vulnerable, but all he'd done was increase their trouble.

"Nico would have gone there whether he went with you to that interview or not. And he'll be fine," she assured him.

Ben finally looked at Emma. He realized that he believed her. Emma was good at her job. Better than he'd ever known. She barked commands so Ben could be the hands treating Nico. Emma was the woman he wanted to spend the rest of his life with. She was the woman he wanted to mother his children. She was the woman that he wanted to love and cherish forever. She was the one.

She was always the one. He only hoped he hadn't realized it too late.

He forced the corners of his lips to turn up. The tightness in his throat only allowed two words to escape. "Thank you."

The thirty-minute drive stretched for an eternity. An eternity of self-examination. Judgment. Guilt. Shame.

Would the slope have stayed open if Ben hadn't taken Hank's side? If Ben had published his suspicions—that Hank's sourness sprouted from displeasure and inconvenience and not a concern for the well-being of the kids—could this have been avoided? Had Ben allowed his personal bias to influence his handling of the story? Had he committed the unforgivable sin for a reporter? A grunt came from the back of his throat.

"It's okay to be angry."

Ben stared straight ahead. He flexed his grip on the steering wheel, and the throbbing ache in his jaw stretched to the base of his ear. Was it okay to be angry at God? He didn't dare look her way. If he did, she might see the wreckage of his soul. He could feel her gaze boring a hole into his profile.

"It's possible to be angry and not sin."

He swallowed, but it refused to go down.

Emma's eyes drifted closed, and her head tilted back against the seat, but she continued to speak. "You're hardwired to know some things are just wrong. I love that about you. You give a voice to the weak. But—" Her eyes opened and found his. "You don't need to fight God on this. You're angry, so be angry. But take it to God. Cry out for help and comfort. He'll fight for Nico."

Deep inside, Ben knew she was right. He was angry at God because God was the only one powerful enough to impart any kind of change, and it felt like He wasn't doing anything. God *allowed* this trial. Chose it. Ordained it. None of it was outside his control. In a way that Ben couldn't understand, this was part of God's plan. That knowledge didn't sit well because it wasn't what Ben would have chosen. How did a person accept hardship and sorrow from God's hand? It wasn't possible.

Except his parents had.

Not only did they accept it, but they forgave the doctor who, in a moment of haste, made a decision that nearly destroyed their family.

Ben's stomach rolled. Was his faith strong enough to love and forgive like that? What if the path grew so hard and lonely that he stopped walking? He gave Emma a side glance. Her eyes remained closed, but her presence beside him was proof he didn't need to walk any path alone.

Ben steered the vehicle into the hospital parking lot. He stopped at the guardrail to push the button for a parking ticket. It gave him something to do besides look at Emma. She was so sure about God. So confident in her faith. But she didn't experience what he did. She didn't know what it was like to pray and pray and pray and pray for God to fix something gone terribly wrong and for

Him to delay. She didn't know that God could, but He sometimes didn't. And Ben refused to voice his deepest fear. What if God didn't? Could Ben survive?

Instead of asking his questions, he parked the car. "I'm getting you a wheelchair." When Emma didn't argue, his heart hammered against his ribs. He hurried back, helped her into the chair, and pushed her through the emergency doors.

"Nico will be in the children's department by now," Emma said.

Ben's gait hitched. The children's department. He hadn't set foot in that wing of the hospital in over fifteen years. The morbid plot twist soured his stomach. God placed the fate of Nico in the same department that destroyed Ben and Claire's childhood.

"Ben?" Emma's tone lifted in a question.

She didn't know. He hadn't told her the rest of the story. He hadn't told her how the hospital had made everything worse. He pointed her chair in the right direction and started walking. It was time to face his demons.

Chapter Twelve

Emma squinted at the person hurrying down the corridor. She remembered that authoritative strut from when she worked at the hospital. *Thank you, Lord!* Reuben would tell her what was going on. "Reuben!"

Dr. Reuben O'Neil stopped in his tracks so suddenly that Ben yanked back on the wheelchair to prevent ramming the back of the man's heels. The motion set a wave of pain through her.

"Emma?" The whites of Reuben's eyes popped against his dark skin. "What happened to you?"

"I had a run-in with a sledding hill." She tried to laugh, but it fell flat.

"Are you okay?" Reuben's attention flicked behind her.

Right. Ben. Where were her manners? "I'll be fine once I get another dose of painkillers. Reuben, this is

Ben. Ben, Reuben and I worked together when I nursed here."

Reuben's eyes widened further at Ben's name. Emma's cheeks heated. He must remember her gushing about Ben. She had hoped he'd forgotten, or at least wouldn't have made the connection until after she and Ben had moved on. The men shook hands, sizing each other up. One to see if Ben was worthy of Emma's affections and the other to see if Reuben posed a romantic threat. Any other time, she might find their posturing amusing.

"Do you happen to know where Nico Privett was brought? He just came in."

"The boy in the sledding accident? They took him to get a CT scan."

"And his mom?"

"Went with him." Reuben raised a brow.

"Nico is Ben's nephew."

Understanding softened Reuben's features. He'd always been a compassionate doctor with a warm bedside manner. "For what it's worth, he was alert and talking when they brought him through here. I think he'll be okay."

Ben didn't respond.

Emma twisted around to see his face. The movement shot heat through her shoulder. "Ben?"

The cloudiness in his eyes lifted, and he tried to cover his discomfort with a quick smile.

Reuben watched Ben with the eye of a doctor, assessing, evaluating, and drawing conclusions. He opened his mouth, hesitated, and seemed to reconsider. He turned back to Emma. "I just finished the paperwork on the case you referred. That was a good call, Emma. It couldn't have been an easy one."

"I'm glad she is able to get the help that she needs," she said.

Ben's crazy ring tone shook him from his frozen state. "It's the paper." He excused himself, walking a few steps down the hall.

"The paper? So, he *is* the reporter guy you told me about!" Reuben wiggled his eyebrows.

The warmth in Emma's cheeks intensified until her face felt like it was on fire. When Ben literally fell into her life, the staff at Grander Hospital got an earful when she relayed the story of how he was chasing the Emergence rumors and found her. They practically swooned when Ben and Emma started dating. They'd created a pool on how long it would take to make their romance official. The winner got free coffee for a week.

A page blared over the hospital's loudspeakers.

"That's me." Reuben glanced to where Ben had wandered. "Tell him it was nice to meet him. Hopefully, you and I'll have a chance to catch up soon."

Ben rejoined her just as Reuben disappeared around a corner. "Did he have any more information on Nico?"

"No, but if you wheel me in the direction of imaging, I bet we'll find your sister in the waiting area." Emma pointed the way they needed to go.

The florescent lighting bounced off the pale walls, making her head hurt. They passed a nurses' station. Behind the desk was a whiteboard loaded with specific patient information. A box of latex gloves sat off to the side, and a metal IV stand with an empty saline bag hanging from the hook stood abandoned. No one manned the station. A phone rang, and two call light buttons were flashing.

It was just as she remembered it.

"He was talking about Janelle Holmes, wasn't he?" The tiniest whisper of Ben's breath caressed her earlobe.

Emma didn't have the energy to fight him on this again, not after everything that had happened today. Ben's tone landed like a fresh blow. This was personal for him. It reminded him of the accusations his parents had faced. She knew that now. But reporting suspected cases of abuse was part of her job. An essential part of her job.

"You sent her here," he pressed. "To this hospital?"

She rubbed her right hand gently over her left arm, which she cinched tightly to her body. The tension in her muscles only seemed to amplify the deep ache in her bones. She wrinkled her forehead against a wave of discomfort. Had a nurse been at the station, she might have asked Ben to stop so they could look for more medication.

"All cases come through here. They actually opened a new wing. Dr. Troy Alister runs it. Reuben works for him."

Ben stopped pushing the chair. He spun her chair

around and backed it next to a bench. She clenched her teeth against the momentum. Ben sat, planted his elbows on his knees, and leaned into her space, finally voicing what was really bothering him. "What if you were wrong?"

A family walked by. The little boy skipped, holding his mother's hand, and clutched a stuffed giraffe under his arm. The whoosh of the automatic doors that separated the children's wing from the rest of the hospital opened and closed. On just the other side of the doors, an alarm dinged. Patients walked the halls. Snippets of conversations bled through forced tones of cheer set to the background music of adjusting beds, side rails snapping into place, running water, and the blare of a television.

"I've been trained to look for it. I don't make those calls lightly." Her mind whirled, but she kept her voice as tender as possible. They trod on thin ice, and she didn't want to be the one who broke it from underneath him.

"Why did you have to send her here? Why couldn't it be handled in Sycamore Hill by the people who knew her and care about her?"

Emma puckered her lips. She got enough pushback from outsiders. She didn't need it from him as well. "We couldn't manage it alone. She wasn't fine. She confessed to me. I had a legal obligation to report it. They'll follow her family closely from here. She'll be okay."

Something in Ben cracked as if the ice gave way and plunged him into the freezing water. His features slackened. He disconnected from the moment, forcing her offended feelings to melt into the background. He was going into shock. "Ben." She spoke loudly and with authority. She squeezed his hands. He needed to make a connection. He needed something solid to ground him.

He blinked several times. His eyes sharpened. He was back.

"This department was created specifically for cases like Janelle's. They are good at what they do here. The people in charge care."

"Like God cares?" It came out all scratchy and hoarse. "If God is all-powerful, this only confirms that all power is corrupted." He squeezed his eyes shut and gripped his knees so hard his knuckles whitened. Emma couldn't make sense of his struggle. Ben cheered for the underdog and gave a voice to the voiceless. This was his wheelhouse. Championing a department that gave children a voice should be a no-brainer for him. But something had triggered him, and he didn't want to talk about it.

Couldn't talk about it might be more accurate.

Not even with the woman he said he loved.

"Ben?"

He drew back slightly. Not far enough to be rude, but enough to communicate that he was done talking. For now, anyway.

So instead of pressing him, she deflected. "What did the paper want?"

He relaxed as if he understood her redirection was a

gift to pause the conversation they needed. His fists loosened.

"Some kids came forward. They claimed that Hank relocated some of his garden gnomes near the slopes."

Her good hand went to her throat. Hank did this on purpose? Her stomach turned over. "Why?" It came out all rough and whispery.

Ben shrugged. "To make sledding difficult, I'd guess. To cause an accident that forced their closure. But this seems extreme, even for him."

"I should feel thankful I was the only one to get hurt." Better her than a child.

"Your arm!" Ben jumped to his feet. "You need stronger pain meds."

"Let's find your sister first."

Ben walked at a faster clip, and they followed the yellow footprints on the linoleum floor to the imaging department waiting room. Claire lifted her head as they came in. A cry ripped from her throat. She launched herself across the room and threw her arms around her brother.

"I'm so glad you're here." She pressed her face into his shoulder and muffled the words.

Ben wrapped his arms around her and pulled her in. His body swayed slightly as he held his sister as tenderly as he would a scared child. There was something beautiful about their relationship that made Emma love Ben even more. He was the kind of guy that was all-in, forever.

"What did the doctor say?"

Claire wiped her eyes. "They think he's going to be fine. They are just making sure there is nothing going on under the surface."

"That's good." Ben kissed her forehead. "I'm so sorry."

"Sorry?" Claire's expression registered shock. She completely untangled herself from him. "For what? For finding him? For helping Emma stabilize him while we waited for the ambulance? For being here with me now? What are you sorry for?" She punctuated her questions by ticking off her statements on the fingers of her left hand.

"I'm sorry that you had to come back to this place with Nico. After all we went through, this can't be easy."

It was Claire's turn to hug her brother.

Come back to this place? Emma struggled to connect the dots, but they were spaced too far apart.

"I think this has been harder on you," Claire said. "I don't remember that time as well as you do. And the doctors have been nothing but good to us. It's okay, Ben. It's going to be okay."

"That's what Mom thought."

Claire paled.

Remember that time? That's what Mom thought? Emma pulled from her memory snippets of phrases, conversations, and history, but the pain made it hard to think clearly. Ben's mom never referenced a poor experience with the hospital, and since Emma worked here for the first several months she and Ben dated, there had been plenty of time and opportunities. "I think someone needs to fill me in."

Chapter Thirteen

I t was time. Ben could see it as clear as day. Emma needed to know. And maybe he needed to say it. Deal with it. Finally, and fully.

Ben focused beyond Emma, on the ugly landscape painting hanging on the wall. It'd be easier if he didn't watch her reaction. He detached from the present in a way that made him feel like an observer of the conversation rather than a participant. "When Claire and I were little, I had that fall on the ice. Claire and I were taken into protective custody."

His peripheral vision noted Emma's nodding head. She remembered.

Ben chewed the inside of his cheek. He didn't know if he could do this. He hadn't spoken of this, ever. Not even afterward, when everything wrong was corrected. As corrected as something like this could be. Not to his parents, who tried their best to make him talk about it. Not to Claire, who didn't really remember. Not to the counsellor that his mom made him go to for months. The only way Ben could cope was to stuff it so deep inside that he couldn't feel it anymore.

Except the body and mind didn't work that way. Even if he forced his brain to reject the memories, the body remembered the trauma. The body reacted instinctively. Ben inhaled deeply. Emma waited. Watched. Not pressing or hurrying him along. Just waiting.

"We were taken into protective custody because of the doctor who treated us at this hospital."

Emma pressed the fingertips of her good hand to her lips.

"He was in a hurry. He didn't ask the right questions. And we were separated from our parents for almost a year."

She gasped.

"I was a lot younger," Claire added. She curled herself into her brother's side. "Only a baby, really. So, I don't remember much. Just flashes of visits with Ben."

"Visits? You weren't placed together or with family members?"

"No. But we had scheduled visits."

Emma's lower lip trembled.

"And I remember everything," Ben said.

Emma's blinks got faster and faster. The color drained from her face as she put the puzzle pieces together.

Ben sucked in a grateful breath. He wasn't sure he'd be able to handle her tears on top of all that raged under his skin.

"That's why this place triggered you."

"The doctors didn't listen to me. I told them what happened. But they didn't believe me."

"Tell me." She reached for him. "I'm listening."

Tears he should have cried years ago finally released. Cleansing tears. Healing tears.

"I'd hurt myself on the ice. Cracked my head pretty hard. But my aunt Grace was visiting, and she's a nurse. She looked me over and told my mom I looked fine. We had a regular check-up scheduled in a few days, so she told my mom what to watch for and advised her to loop in the doctor at the check-up."

Emma's head bobbed. She'd heard this part already. The medical community's understandings of concussions had changed so much in the last decade. Things would have been different had it happened today.

"By the time we went to the doctor, the bruises were ugly, but he knew our family. He checked me over and agreed with Aunt Grace. I was fine. But Mom was worried, so he referred us here for a CT scan just to be on the safe side."

Emma rolled her bottom lip between her teeth. Her eyes widened, but she remained silent, letting him get this out.

"The doctors here didn't know us. By the time I saw

them, a bruise had formed on my arm from where my mom grabbed me when I fell. It bothered them."

"A handprint bruise," Emma murmured.

He nodded. She got it. "They reported my injuries as suspicious to Children's Aid, and despite Aunt Grace and the family doctor, things spun out of control. We were taken into care."

Care. He spat the word. Care was the last word he'd use to describe that season of life.

Emma's expression morphed from soft to hard. "Their highest priority is keeping families together. How could something like this happen?"

She'd moved from denial to anger. She'd get to acceptance eventually. If he and Claire could, she would, too. "Mom and Dad had to fight it in court. We had supervised visits with them. Our lawyer kept saying the decision would be reversed. They didn't have a strong case, but it dragged on."

"This should have been a quick fix." Emma's jaw twitched angrily.

Claire wiped her eyes with the back of her hand. "Except no one would own it. Jobs were on the line. Case workers dug into their positions instead of humbly admitting the error."

"They spoke with people who said they saw Mom grab my arm roughly. It got taken out of context, and once certain things had been set into motion, it was nearly impossible to reverse the train. Rulings went against us, and Mom and Dad kept appealing. They nearly went bankrupt. Finally, a judge at the highest level looked over the case, the testimonies given, and my statement, and threw the entire case out of court with sincere apologies to my parents."

Emma exhaled her words. "That's awful."

"Awful doesn't even begin to describe it."

"Afterward," Claire interjected, "Mom struggled to get an appointment with the head of this department to discuss what went wrong. She didn't want this to happen to anyone else."

"They kept refusing to meet," Ben said. "They put her off for months. They were sure she was going to ambush them with some sort of civil suit."

"But Mom forgave them." Claire's eyes shone. "She laid out exactly how the series of bad decisions impacted our family. She placed the blame with them, acknowledging that at any point they could have humbly realized their error and turned the tide, but they dug in. And she forgave them, saying she had to because if she didn't, the resentment would kill her. This is where Ben got his passion for helping the powerless and exposing corruption."

Ben dipped his head at his sister's praise.

"I need to introduce you to Dr. Troy."

His mouth slackened. After spilling his guts out, all she could think about was introducing him to the head of the department that destroyed his life?

"Claire," Emma asked. "Can you roll me to the desk?"

Claire pushed Emma toward reception. Ben cradled his head in his hands. He curled inward. Heat prickled his chest. It was too much.

A page requesting Dr. Troy to imaging sounded over the loudspeakers.

Lord, I don't know if I can do this.

But his parents did it. In fact, what they did was even harder.

I need you, Lord.

A clean-shaven man in his mid to late forties approached the desk. The receptionist pointed at the threesome.

"Emma?" Surprise colored his voice. "What happened?"

She gave a succinct summary of her accident.

"You look like you're in pain."

"I am," she admitted.

Yet she insisted on doing this first. Helping him before addressing her needs.

Dr. Troy returned to the reception desk, said a few words to the nurse, and then returned. "They are pulling your chart. I've asked them to bring you more pain meds."

"Thank you."

"What can I do for you? I'm sure that's not why you called me to imaging."

"I want you to meet Ben."

Dr. Troy tilted his head slightly to the side. "It's nice to meet you, Ben."

"Ben Sawyer," Emma added softly. "And his sister, Claire."

Dr. Troy did a double take. Understanding fell over him that Ben didn't get. Why was his name so significant to this man? The doctor straightened to his full height and offered Ben his hand.

Ben saw nothing but sincerity in the man's gaze. He stood to accept his offered handshake hesitantly, not sure what was happening.

"Your family is legend here."

His family?

"The hospital was determined to learn from its mistakes. To be what your mother suggested, humble and teachable."

"You know my mother?"

"Not personally, but she had a key role in shaping the job description for my position at the hospital."

"My mom?" Claire appeared just as flabbergasted as he felt.

"My job is to investigate suspected cases of abuse. I still have to report to Family and Children Services, but this policy ensures a fuller report that includes family history and hospital visits from neighboring communities or a lack of hospital visits to neighboring communities. It came into effect after your family's crisis and because of your family's experience."

Because, like junkies looking for a fix, abusers spread out their care to avoid detection.

"We are determined to never put a family through what you endured again."

"Why wouldn't Mom tell us this?" Claire whispered.

"I think she might have tried." Ben's face felt slack. Memories of his mom trying to talk with him about that time in their life filled him. "I always shut her down. I couldn't talk about it. I couldn't go there."

Regret slammed against his ribs. Could he have found the peace he needed long ago if he'd just been brave enough to have the conversation? He not only refused to talk about that trauma with his parents, but he also insisted on moving forward as if nothing had happened.

"You're treating Janelle?"

"I can't talk about a patient, but children like Janelle are why these services are still needed. *You* are why these services need checkpoints and real people reviewing the documents."

Ben's head swam. He sank onto the bench, and the vinyl seat whooshed. He could hardly think. His mom, probably scarred just as deeply as he was, came back to the hospital, to the same people that nearly destroyed their family, and worked alongside them to better their policies.

Because that was who she was.

"Sometimes the system fails, but it's doing its best." Dr. Troy held out his hand again to Ben. But this time, it wasn't in greeting. This time, Ben knew, without a doubt, it was an apology and a promise. An apology for all his family endured and a commitment to never again let something like that happen on his watch.

Ben accepted his offering, and as he did, the rock that had been permanently lodged in his gut dissolved. Instead of leaving Ben empty, it made him feel whole. Complete. And hopeful.

Chapter Fourteen

Kathryn zipped up the back of Emma's dress, and Emma's cheeks burned. She couldn't believe the number of things she could not do one-handed—intimate things that required her friends to step up and be the hands and feet of Jesus. But Emma was home now, and she was so grateful to be in her condo, even if it meant giving up her independence for a time.

Lola, her cat, curled up and warmed her feet most nights, making everything feel almost normal. As per the doctor's orders, Emma had taken it easy since leaving the hospital. Kathryn, Claire, Meg, Gloria, and a few other women from the community created a schedule and rotated staying with her. But today was Meg and Eli's wedding, and nothing was going to stop Emma from standing with her friend.

Kathryn turned Emma around and looked her over from top to bottom. "Perfect."

Emma grinned as she moved to sit on the bed. "As perfect as a gown accessorized by a sling can be."

Kathryn rifled through Emma's closet, talking over her shoulder. "I made an interesting discovery when sorting through my videos of the slopes."

"Something better than my blooper reel?"

Kathryn held out a pair of close-toed strappy heels. "These ones?"

"Yes."

"Better isn't the word I would use." Kathryn pulled out a newspaper and handed it to Emma before kneeling at her feet to fiddle with the ankle straps. "It's folded open to the right place. Read Ben's article."

Emma ran her gaze over the page. Her pulse hiccupped. "They charged Hank?"

"With mischief." Kathryn sat back on her heels after buckling the shoes. "Now, what purse would you like?"

Emma couldn't think about purses. All she could think about were the snippets of memory starting to come back about the day of the accident. Hank bent over her, crying. Hank, telling her to stay strong. That help was coming. That he was sorry.

She never heard the apology as a confession. No one did until they discovered Hank's actions. She'd seen him as a compassionate man grieving the actuality of a catastrophe that he'd predicted would happen.

Kathryn held up two purses.

"The black one, please." Emma motioned to the

black purse with a gold chain strap, and Kathryn returned the brown one to the shelf in the closet.

"The rumor was Hank moved the garden gnomes to the slope to make parents think it was too dangerous for their kids. His plan was to be out there first thing in the morning to discover them." Kathryn put air quotes around the word discover. "He wanted to find them in front of an audience before anyone went down and got hurt."

"But we arrived early—"

"—for my morning show," Kathryn finished. "I hope it helps a little to know that he didn't intend to hurt anyone." Kathryn slipped an arm around Emma's waist and aided her to her feet. "What about your hair? Up or down?"

"Down is fine. It's easier." Emma followed Kathryn into the bathroom, where a hot curling iron waited. "You said video. What video?"

"I had arrived at the slopes long before you to film the sunrise and some B reel. Turns out, I caught Hank in the background without knowing it."

"I still can't believe it," Emma murmured. Hank was a bit grizzly at church, but he wasn't malicious. But when a person wanted something badly enough, most were willing to sin to achieve it. Hank was no different.

What a troubling idea.

She continued to scan the article. "The town is reopening the slopes?"

"Yes, but with some changes." Kathryn ran the iron

through Emma's hair, creating a cascade of curls down her back. "They're discussing a dedicated parking lot and vendor area to relocate the chaos away from the homes on the cul-de-sac. They are also putting in an outdoor ice rink."

Emma had just reached that part in Ben's article. "Why? We have the pond."

"Since our winter temps fluctuate so much, they wanted a space they could guarantee was safe to skate on. Plus, they can run an outdoor ice hockey league in the winter and ball hockey in the summer."

"I feel like I've been laid up forever to have missed all of this." But really, it wasn't that long. It only felt that way because Ben had been so busy with the paper that they hadn't had the chance for a long and lingering visit. They hadn't even unpacked all the emotions he must be feeling about the hospital.

About her.

Them.

A part of her still feared she had pushed the only man she ever loved away. But tonight, they were going to the wedding. Tonight, they would chat. Finally. About the things that mattered.

"You haven't read to the end yet, have you?" Kathryn's eyes twinkled.

Emma's gaze hopped to the last paragraph. "It says part one of two."

Kathryn had that look that meant she knew something Emma didn't. Before Emma could ask, the doorbell rang. Kathryn hurried out of the room.

The heavy footfalls in the hallway were not the light step of her friend. The stride was all wrong. "Kathryn?"

"Try again." Ben's chuckle settled over Emma like hot fudge on a sundae. Delicious, comfortable, and warm.

"You're early!" She jumped up from her perch on the edge of the bed. She looked past Ben and down the empty hallway. "Where's Kathryn?"

"She said something about taking Lola out front."

Emma was probably the only person in the world that walked her cat on a leash.

"What do you think?" Emma spun for Ben as he let out a low, appreciative whistle. Heat filled her cheeks.

"First, you look amazing. Second, do you need help with anything?" Ben leaned a shoulder against her bedroom doorframe, keeping both feet firmly in the hallway.

Pleasure over his compliment rippled through her body. "I'll be out in a minute." She was ready now, but she needed a minute to compose herself. Something about Ben standing in her hall, looking at her the way he was looking at her, made her feel dizzy inside.

She found Ben in the kitchen, settled on one of her horribly uncomfortable barstools. Uncomfortable but stylish. A newspaper was spread out on the island.

"What's this?" She nodded toward the paper.

"Part two of that article series. It goes to press tomorrow, but I got an early copy for you."

She wrinkled her forehead.

"Read it." He nudged it closer to her.

Emma slid onto the stool beside Ben. His eagerness aroused nervousness and excitement equally. The weight of Ben's gaze on her profile never lifted as she moved her eyes over the article. Her heart thumped in her chest. Her eyes moved slowly over the words, taking in each phrase. Somehow, she knew deep in her bones that this moment was special. Important. Worthy of her time.

"Read it aloud," he prompted. A notch between his eyes deepened.

Gooseflesh crept across her arms. She cleared her throat. "Normally, you read my article above the fold. I report on breaking news, local news, and everything that impacts our town. But today, I'm in a new section of the paper, the letter to the editor section, because what I have to say is not just facts from a neutral reporter. It's about my heart, which holds a definite bias.

"When a man reaches a fork in the road, he has to decide. Will he follow his heart or follow the job? For as long as I can remember, I wanted to be a journalist at a big paper. I wanted to be a voice for the voiceless. I wanted to right wrongs and fight injustice. This deeply-rooted need drove every decision until the day I fell (literally) for Emma Powles." Her swollen throat pinched off her words.

Emma cleared her throat, but it didn't help. She tried

again, but the frog remained. Ben gently took the paper from her hand and continued the narration. The pages trembled. "Emma showed me what it meant to release my burden to the Lord. She showed me that my worth wasn't tied to my performance. She showed me that the only One able to right the wrongs we face on the earth had to die in order to do it and rose to new life to secure eternity for those who believe."

Her eyes filled. Her voice turned husky, "If you make my makeup run—"

Ben's smile was delicious and slow, creeping across his features a millimeter at a time. She willed her focus from his lips to his words. "I was offered my dream job as a result of my coverage on Emergence and the town battle for the Sycamore Slopes. But in a strange moment of clarity, I realized I already had everything I had ever dreamed of right here in Sycamore Hill. In this community. In Emma Powles. In my faith in the Lord."

Now Ben's voice hitched. As his words thickened and grew rougher, Emma wiped the dampness from her cheeks. No wonder Kathryn insisted on waterproof mascara. Emma's fragile grip broke when Ben slid off the stool and bent one knee to the floor. Her belly quivered, and she pressed her hand against it. She couldn't breathe.

Ben continued to read from his position at her feet. "Emma Powles is my best friend, and today, I hope that I can say, my soon-to-be-wife. Emma Powles, will you marry me?"

Emma's tears dampened her upper lip. Her gaze

moved over this man who had stolen her heart from the day he landed in a heap in the middle of her living room. She loved his compassion for the lost, his strong sense of justice, and his willingness to do anything for the people he loved. It was a privilege to love him.

She slid from the stool and stooped over, threading the fingers of one hand through the back of his hair. She pressed their foreheads together.

He cupped her cheek with his palm, and she leaned into his warmth. Her eyes fell closed, and she whispered one word. "Yes."

One Month Later

Chapter Fifteen

A bloodcurdling shriek sliced through the frosty air. Ben lifted his camera to his eye and peered through the lens, rotating the dial. He focused on the slope, newly re-opened and heavily monitored, and snapped a cluster of images. The town council had discussed the recent events and decided to reopen the area, but with significant changes. Some changes would come into effect over the next year, and some were immediate, like the small portion of space designated as the vendor area. It redirected the traffic away from the residences.

The Sycamore and Martin families generously donated the funds for the project named the *Sycamore Skate and Sled Park*. A billboard displayed their future plans, which included a manufactured rink set in the organic outdoors to replace the pond skating, holiday music chiming from loudspeakers connected to the rink, and a variety of outdoor vendors. The town implemented a schedule for the park. The opening hours of nine in the morning until nine in the evening ensured the surrounding community had enough quiet.

The temporary changes seemed to satisfy Hank, who stood in line for a corn dog. Hank gave a nearby child a thumbs-up as they ran past. The old grouch had come a long way. The grinchiness of Hank softened as Emma took a page from Ben's mom's book and insisted on sitting down with the person who'd hurt her. Hank tried to avoid Emma, but she wouldn't let up. And when they finally got together, she was able to communicate in person what had already transpired in her heart. She forgave Hank.

In the end, Emma and Hank brought the idea of the Skate and Sled Park to the town council together. And as they told their story of a neighborhood fed up with the chaos, they also presented the solution: a creative reimagining of the landscape, enforced hours of operation and giving the locals a voice in the design.

Pop Up Food Vendors are a Hit with Locals. Ben mentally filed the potential headline.

Ben peered through the camera lens again, getting a clearer view of the kids. Oliver skated between his mom and his Uncle Jackson. As Ben focused the lens, it sharpened Jackson's features. The man was in love with Kim. It was evident to everybody. What was it going to take for them to see it? Oliver's feet slipped and slid, but Oliver remained upright. The couple cheered for his success.

"I do it! I do it!" Oliver's delight warmed Ben's insides.

Ben snapped another cluster of pictures.

On the far side of the park, Janelle Holmes shrieked. The Holmes family had a long way to go, but they were working with Family and Children Services. Janelle's parents were in counselling while Janelle lived with an aunt. They were committed to making better choices and earning back the privilege of raising their daughter.

A happy ending appeared as a possibility. Ben hoped they'd reach it. As he repacked his satchel, he mulled over his life choices. Staying in Sycamore Hill no longer felt like settling for second best. He wasn't resigned to it. He chose it. The dream had been within reach, but he decided to reach for something else. Something better. Marrying Emma, raising a family, and supporting her as she ran her clinic.

"Uncle Ben!" Nico waved as he raced toward the hill. A long blue sled attached to a thin yellow rope bounced behind him.

And watching Nico grow up. Helping Claire. Being here for his aging parents. Becoming a dad.

"I thought I'd find you here." Emma lifted her face for his usual kiss, but he bypassed her freckled cheek and brushed her lips with his. The tension in his body evaporated, replaced with a settled peace.

"Where else would I be?"

Emma turned into his arms, and he briefly tightened his hold. She fit perfectly against him. His arms slipped from her waist, and he scooped up her hands. He tugged her toward the bench.

She snuggled into his side. "Are you done work yet?"

Even if he wasn't done, he wouldn't miss the chance to sit with his girl. They wouldn't be skating. Emma was still careful with her collarbone. It would take six to eight weeks to heal and at least the same period again to regain full use of it. He tucked his satchel into one of the cubbies built under the benches. "I'm all yours."

"We made it!" Meg huffed a bit as she and Eli joined Ben and Emma. "Are Owen and Gloria coming?"

"Any minute."

Meg and Eli swapped their boots for skates, and their banter filled Ben to overflowing. It was surreal to think he'd almost walked away from this. Gloria and Owen joined them. Ben and Emma laughed, watching their friends on the ice. They even tried their hand at crack the whip. Kathryn filmed from the edge of the rink. They'd probably show up on her Sycamore Hill at Sunrise show.

Jackson zoomed up behind Kim. He gestured to Oliver, and Kim nodded her consent. Jackson scooped up the boy from behind and tossed him into the air. Oliver shrieked with delight.

"Careful," Emma called out. "I don't want to have to get out my medical bag."

Jackson lowered Oliver until his blades grazed the ice's surface. He supported his weight, and they lapped his mother again.

"Do it again," Oliver giggled.

Ben's gaze returned to Emma. He couldn't wait to toss his children into the air. To skate and play and not be consumed with fear that there would be an accident.

Because accidents happened.

But his God reigned.

One Sycamore
Sunday

BOOK 4

Follow Jackson and Kim's story in One Sycamore Sunday. Kim's day begins like any other until one terrifying moment changes everything.

CHAPTER ONE - ONE SYCAMORE SUNDAY

"Oliver!" Kim Jansen tapped her booted foot on the hardwood floor at the bottom of the short staircase. If he didn't hurry, they'd be late for church again. A crash and a thud came from behind his closed bedroom door. He was probably looking for something that he *just couldn't live without*. Oliver came by his flair for the dramatic honestly. His father, Hayden, had always been a showman.

Bitterness filled her mouth, as it always did when she thought of Hayden. She swallowed hard and tightened her grip on the banister. Hayden couldn't interfere again. Jackson, his twin brother, made sure of it.

The brothers were identical in every physical way. They shared the same rugged good looks, blond, wavy hair, and piercing blue eyes. But that's where the likeness stopped. Jackson was as good as Hayden was evil. And Jackson had sacrificed his relationship with his twin to bring Oliver home. For that, she'd be forever in his debt.

But he didn't do it for her. It was for Oliver.

Her midsection flip-flopped. At least that's what she told herself. "Oli-verrrr!" She forced cheerfulness into her tone. There had to be some sort of brother code forbidding a guy from dating his twin brother's ex.

Oliver popped through his bedroom doorway and into the hall. She couldn't help but smile as her three-year-old son lazily took the stairs one step at a time, dragging his stuffed bunny behind him as if they had all day. She'd given him the bunny last month for his birthday, and he hadn't let go of it since.

The rabbit's head thumped on each step.

"I coming." When he finally reached the bottom, he stopped in front of her and lifted his face.

She bent and kissed his cheek. "We need to motor, my little love." She ruffled his hair, her caress dulling the urgency of her words. So, they were late for church. In the grand scheme of life, that was a small thing. It was only a little more than a year ago that she would have given anything to have her son back under her roof, even a lifetime of last-to-arrive-at-church Sundays.

She shook loose the memory of their lost time. It might be good to remember but it wasn't healthy to linger. Lingering birthed bitterness, and bitterness about the parental abduction that separated her from Oliver for fourteen months never led her to a good spiritual place. She lifted her chin, sucking in air though her nose. She'd forgiven Hayden. As much as a person could forgive someone that wasn't sorry. She grabbed her bag and slung it over her shoulder, refusing to let guilt take root. Forgiveness was a decision, but it was also a process. She was working on it.

"Have everything for Sunday school?" she asked.

Oliver attached the Velcro of his shoes and beamed at her. The shoes were on the wrong feet, and she should probably tell him to put on boots, but she'd take the win of him putting on some sort of footwear.

"Ready!" Oliver lifted his arms for her to pick him up.

"Not quite, buddy. You need a jacket." She handed him his puffy orange winter coat. The February chill had dropped below normal temperatures for their region, and their friendly groundhog had recently announced six more weeks of winter.

She helped his arms into his coat and zipped up the front, ignoring the way he swatted her fingers because he wanted to do it himself. He wedged his bunny into his armpit and tugged on mittens and a hat.

A light wind picked up the dusty snow and stung their cheeks as they trudged to the car. The cold air made it hurt to breathe. The scent of pine from the trees that lined the property grew stronger. It only took another five minutes to get Oliver buckled into his car seat and finally start toward church. Eight-thirty. Not too bad. They might slip in just as the first song started.

She turned on the Christian radio station and hummed along to a familiar tune about God's goodness. Oliver chattered to himself, holding the bunny up to the window so the rabbit could see the passing scenery. "Unca Jackson?"

"Not today, love. He's working." Jackson was the only police presence in Sycamore Hill, and he worked every other Sunday. On his off days, he kept his phone on him for emergencies, but today was a work day. Kim still had to pinch herself to believe that Jackson had uprooted his entire life and career to relocate to Sycamore Hill and be part of Oliver's life. No one had ever sacrificed for her like that before.

The wind iced the morning fog. A small SUV emerged from the haziness behind her. It crept closer and closer to her bumper. Thick flakes fell from the sky, and her lack of traction meant the compacted snow pressed into ice under the vehicle's tires. She tapped her brakes, but the guy behind her didn't take the hint. He rode her backside like he was hitched to her bumper. She pressed her lips together and squinted in the rearview mirror. She didn't recognize the man, and he was too close for her to see his license plate, not that it would help. It wasn't like she could report him to Jackson for following too closely.

She flicked her gaze back to the road in front of her. Red lights. She hit the brakes. The wheels slid, and the antilock system kicked in. It pumped the brakes. Still, the back end swung left and then right, and then left again. She cranked the steering wheel the opposite way. Each time, the arch got bigger and bigger as she tried to steer them out of it.

"Mommy!" Oliver screamed.

The vehicle spun three-hundred and sixty degrees and skidded across the centre line. "No, no, no, no, no!"

By some small miracle, there was no oncoming traffic. She managed to avoid hitting the car that had braked so suddenly, but she couldn't avoid the ditch.

She stood on the brake pedal. The front tires turned but the back tires didn't. They spun, and then finally gripped the road. She yanked left as hard as she could. The car shuddered as they hit the ditch. Loose snow absorbed their arrival. Everything stopped.

Oliver!

She twisted. Eyes spread wide. Pale skin. Bunny clutched in his fisted hand. But he was in one piece. *Thank you, Lord.*

"We're okay, honey." She rubbed his knee. A hum echoed deep in her ears. She exhaled, and inch by inch the tightness in her neck and shoulders lessened. *They were okay. They were okay. They were okay.*

A giant tear slid down Oliver's cheek.

Out. They needed to get out.

The ditch wasn't deep, but the overnight snowfall had filled it. There was no way she'd be able to open Oliver's passenger side door, but she could open hers.

The other drivers had stopped, and three men hurried toward her. She forced herself to inhale slowly and deeply. They were okay, too. *Thank you, God!*

"Are you all right?" The men reached the car and huddled around the driver's door.

"We're fine. Are you all okay?" They appeared unharmed. She unbuckled and retrieved her purse, which had slid to the floor on the passenger side. "I'll call the police—"

The door jerked open, and her purse was snatched from her hands. Before she could speak, the man tossed it into the snowbank.

"What are you doing?" Wind stung her cheeks. Incomprehension blurred the edges. She looked to the other men, expecting them to intervene, but they had opened the back door and were fumbling with Oliver's buckles. Her mind denied what was unfolding. This wasn't real. It couldn't be real. Her ears roared.

"Mommy!"

Shock transformed into panic. She lunged toward Oliver, slapping at the men's hands. A growl erupted from the deepest place in her soul. She'd kill them to protect her son.

A sharp pain split her cheek. Metallic blood filled her mouth, the acrid tang of blood. What was happening? WHAT WAS HAPPENING? All she could see, smell, and hear was Oliver's fear. Her fear.

"Mommy!"

A cloudiness took over. Another blow landed, and it flung her into the passenger seat. Then the sound of pounding feet and shouting.

Terror in Oliver's voice. "Don't hurt my mommy!"

She only caught bits and pieces. Oliver flailing his arms and legs. A rip. A wail. They pulled him from the car. She fought for consciousness. Oliver's cries were the only sounds that penetrated the roar in her ears. It was the only thing she could focus on.

The men were bigger and stronger. An angry bark emitted from one, and Oliver's cries faded. Kim struggled to right herself. She blinked rapidly but still couldn't see straight. Her cheek stung. Her body ached. She was wedged in a seat, her breathing shallow. Her heart beat against her forehead. The car was too quiet. It was a screaming quiet that filled her mind and exploded from her lips.

And the radio played as if everything right in the world hadn't gone wrong. The artist crooned about a good, good God.

Kim fumbled with the door handle. Her panicked hands refused to work. Finally, she gave up and pounded the glass. "You're not good. You're not a good God. Not a good Father!" She pressed her forehead to the glass and wept. A keening. Not again. Hayden wouldn't do this to her. God wouldn't let it happen.

But Hayden had done it before. And God didn't do a thing to stop it.

Oliver. She had to think of Oliver.

Her mind cleared. She blinked. The hum of a thousand caffeinated drinks shot through her body. The passenger door was wedged into the snowbank. That was why she couldn't open it. She clawed her way to the driver's side and out. A blast of cold hit like the arctic winter. The sting of a slap to her face. Her boots sank into the snow past her ankles. Was Oliver on foot? He only had his shoes on.

She should have made him wear his boots. She should have insisted.

She scrambled up the snowbank on her hands and knees. Snow slowly filled the tracks from where the two

SUVs had driven away. Minutes. Only a few minutes had passed.

They were gone. Oliver was gone.

Her legs shook uncontrollably and gave way. No. She pushed herself up. Oliver needed her to fight.

"Oliver!" Her crawl morphed into a run. Then she was sprinting through the snow to a dark spot on the white bank. If she didn't stop moving, she'd find them. The toe of her boot jammed into an icy lip, and she lurched forward. Cold shot up her arms as her hands tunneled through the snow.

Oliver's bunny. The ear was torn and dangled by threads. She clutched it against her chest. "Oliver!"

It started as a normal Sunday, but one horrifying moment changed everything forever.

When a group of men abduct her son, Kim Jansen turns to the only person she can trust—Jackson McGregor. Officer McGregor would trade his life for the boy, but it's not McGregor the kidnappers want. They want a woman Kim helped disappear, and they've taken Kim's son as leverage. As McGregor races to save the boy, Kim faces an impossible choice—protect her friend or save her child.

One Sycamore Sunday is a high-stakes, fast-paced romance.

Order now!

To Sweet Beginnings in Sycamore Hill

FREE: SERIES INTRODUCTION

Sign up for Stacey's newsletter and see how it all began for the couples you love from Sycamore Hill.

When a whistleblower speaks up, she tips the first domino of a twenty-four-hour chain reaction on the eve of Sycamore Hill's most important holiday event. A baker gets a career-making opportunity, a reporter chases the truth, a woman faces her greatest fear, and a lost child returns as the dominos continue to fall. The residents of Sycamore Hill approach a new year, and five couples celebrate sweet beginnings filled with endless possibilities in this short story sequence.

OWEN AND GLORIA: THURSDAY 2:00 P.M.

Sycamore Hill's prodigal daughter returns, shaking up the small town, righting a wrong, and finding the faith and family she'd lost along the way.

Gloria hasn't returned to Sycamore Hill since her university declared her guilty of cheating. She'd lost more than her home that day; she'd lost her faith in humanity. But when a questionable drug study with ties to the university endangers the residents of a Sycamore Hill ministry, Gloria can no longer remain quiet. She returns to town, and Owen—the town's unmarried pastor and the only person who believed in her innocence—helps her to finally and truly come home.

ETHAN AND KATHRYN: THURSDAY 11:59 P.M.

When you mix two former sweethearts, one missing recipe, and a dash of secrecy, what do you get? A recipe for romance!

Kathryn took something that belongs to Ethan. Correction. It belongs to his family. Taking it back isn't stealing, and letting himself into Kathryn's house to get it is not breaking and entering if he has a key. However, Kathryn's not a thief. She'd found Ethan's recipe. But when her actions threaten to spoil Ethan's bakery, they whip up a solution on Kathryn's internet morning show, Sycamore Hill at Sunrise.

BEN AND EMMA: FRIDAY 3:00 A.M.

God closes a door, but He opens a skylight, entwining Ben and Emma's future in the twilight hours of a winter's eve.

Nursing school made dating impossible for Emma, and now that she finally has time to think about a relationship, the pickings are slim, especially in a small town like Sycamore Hill. She's begun petitioning the Lord to drop Mr. Right into her life, ideally before a black-tie gala fundraiser. She can't bear the idea of attending alone —again.

When Ben—a local reporter—chases the scoop of a lifetime, he falls painfully into Emma's kitchen. With a whistleblower about to rip the lid off a scandal that'll put the small town on the map, Ben needs Emma's help to follow the career-making lead and protect the residents of Sycamore Hill.

ELI AND MEG: FRIDAY 7:35 A.M.

At some point, a girl has to stop running and fight.

Eli is willing to help Meg, but how can he fight an unknown enemy?

Eli and Meg trained together every morning to prepare for an annual road race. When Meg is uncharacteristically late on race day, Eli knows in his gut that something is wrong. He finds Meg facing her greatest fear, and Eli thrusts himself between her and an aggressive animal. However, when Meg passes up an opportunity to escape to safety, he realizes no one in Sycamore Hill really knows Meg at all.

JACKSON AND KIM: FRIDAY, 6:00 P.M. AND SATURDAY MORNING

Kim didn't want to like her ex's twin brother, but how could she not like the man returning her abducted son?

Kim doesn't have the mental headspace to host the black-tie gala on the eve of her abducted son's homecoming, but she must. As she grapples with conflicting emotions about the morning reunion, she clings to the message of Christmas: God with us.

Returning his nephew to Canada destroyed Jackson's relationship with his twin brother. And after all his brother had put Kim through, she might not welcome the continued presence of Jackson or his parents in Sycamore Hill. Sorting out the legalities won't be easy, but the right thing rarely is. Jackson will do what is right, whatever the personal cost, trusting the message of the season.

Sign up for Stacey's newsletter and read for free! If you're already subscribed, input the email you subscribed with and you'll be able to download the ebook.

The Sycamore Standoff

BOOK 1

Eli and Meg's story continues in The Sycamore Standoff, where Meg wants independence and Eli wants her affections. They'll have to face her past for any chance of a future.

A man with a plan, a woman with a past, and a thorny adventure called love.

Welcome to Sycamore Hill, where hearts mend, redemption is within reach, and love's blossoms endure even the harshest storms.

Landscape Architect Meg Gilmore's past resurfaces, threatening the harmony she's fought to cultivate. She's forced to confront the powerful family of Eli Martin, a friend she thought she could trust. With a 250-year-old tree—the very heart of Sycamore Hill—at stake, Meg and Eli's goals intertwine. For now.

Eli's roots run as deep as the ancient tree, and his noble intentions clash with familial expectations. He tries to help Meg—the first woman to see beyond his wealth and status—but only jeopardizes their future. Will Eli and Meg find their way out of the weeds and let love bloom, or will their secrets tear them apart?

Explore themes of trust, forgiveness, community, and the resilience of love in this stirring tale of redemption. Fans of Karen Kingsbury and Deborah Raney will love The Sycamore Standoff. Buy now before the price changes!

Order your copy!

Gloria and Owen's story continues in His Sycamore Sweetheart, where Gloria is willing to do anything to salvage her reputation except the one thing the community demands.

She wants acceptance. He wants approval. They get a wardrobe malfunction, confusion, and a church scandal.

Gloria Sycamore isn't looking for a hero's welcome, but she does expect a friendly one when she returns to Sycamore Hill. After all, she is a Sycamore, and she's dating the local minister. But the community questions her commitment to her faith, the town, and their pastor —who they are not keen on sharing.

Pastor Owen Mason loves his church, but his parishioners weigh in on everything. When push comes to shove, Owen discovers that he can't please them both. Will he be forced to choose between his congregation and his heart?

Gloria sets out to prove herself worthy, navigating the messy (and sometimes hilarious) muddy water of dating in the public eye, where nothing is private, and everything is up for debate.

Small-town charm, laugh-out-loud moments, and a captivating love story guarantee His Sycamore Sweetheart will make you cheer for Gloria and Owen as they fumble their way to true love.

Order your copy!

A Sycamore Secret

BOOK 5

Ethan's custom coffee blend pairs with Kathryn's social media following in A Sycamore Secret, brewing a latte of trouble when Tiff returns to Sycamore Hill. Read the stunning conclusion to the Sycamore Hill series.

His custom coffee blend, paired with her social media following, brews a latte of trouble.

When the Audience Favorite Awards include Kathryn Withers's independent web show as a finalist, the internet trolls slither out from under their bridges. Kathryn livestreams daily, growing her following and improving her chances of winning, but trending on social media backfires. The generated buzz connects the arrival of an unwelcome guest in Sycamore Hill to a shameful secret in Kathryn's past. A secret she'd do *almost* anything to keep hidden.

Ethan Roberts invested every penny in expanding his bakery, The Muffin Man, to include on-site coffee roasting. When Kathryn streams from his location, the increased visibility boosts his confidence that everything he has ever wanted is at his fingertips. But the frenzied online comments and lingering paparazzi prove that mixing a tenacious morning show host, an entrepreneurial baker, and a decade-old secret only percolates trouble.

A Sycamore Secret is filled to the brim with small-town charm, a faith-filled community, and a slow-roasted romance perfectly brewed to a sweet and smooth finish.

Order Now!

Finding the treasure hidden in trials.

Order now!

Do you long for the joy of complete dependence on God yet fear the cost of full surrender? Do you long for unconditional acceptance and love but fear exposing your heart? Do you long for solid peace, absolute trust, and contentment amidst alarming circumstances but fear that those circumstances might shatter your soul?

We fight God for control of our lives because we worry that

suffering will overwhelm us. We want a future free of risk, hurt, and heartbreak. But God isn't calling us to risk-free lives —He is calling us to surrender. Some of God's greatest blessings are hiding behind those parts of our lives that are most difficult to surrender.

The first edition won the Women's Journey of Faith award. The second edition of Glorious Surrender includes five personal, in-depth study times in the Word to aid in the application and understanding of Scripture.

PRAISE FOR GLORIOUS SURRENDER

In Glorious Surrender, Stacey Weeks writes with transparency about the tension and the transformation that her role as a pastor's wife played in bringing her to the place of ultimate freedom—one who seeks God's glory above all else. She communicates with honesty about the messiness of real life in public ministry and takes readers on a journey through raw life topics including pride, living authentically, finding true rest in the chaos, and spiritual warfare. Her passion for God's glory to preoccupy and transform everyday living accompanies every thought on every page. This book is not just for pastors' wives, it is for women wanting to take a vulnerable look at the sins and deceptions that lurk within their minds and hearts that can stall their progress toward finding true purpose. A must-read!

— ANDREA THOM, AUTHOR OF

RUTH: REDEEMING THE DARKNESS
AND AMOS: COME AWAKE!

Often we sit in our seats and wonder what the life of our pastor is like but forget that there is another person in that relationship that must honour the God-given calling of that man. Glorious Surrender is more than Stacey's story; it is about God's ability to shape any ordinary person into the image of Him.

— KEVIN MILLER, CHURCH ELDER

If you want to glorify God in everything you think, say, and do, I recommend reading Glorious Surrender.

— TAMI SWARTZ, BIBLICAL COUNSELLOR

Acknowledgments

Writing is never a one-person adventure. Despite the hours I live inside my head working on a story or book, countless others invest in the project. I would have never created Sycamore Hill without the encouragement of my writing friends in the Brantford Writers Group. Thank you, Karen, Sandy, Heather, Tara, Sandra, and Deirdre for your enthusiasm and belief in me. You believed these characters had more to their stories.

Thank you to an extraordinary editor, Olivia, from LivEdits. You helped tie the threads of this story together. I look forward to our next project together.

About the Author

Stacey is a ministry wife, mother of three teenagers, and a sipper of hot tea with honey. She loves to open the Word of God and share the hope of Christ with women. She is a multi-award-winning author, the primary home-educator of her children, and a frequent conference speaker. Her messages have been described as rich in the truths of Scripture, gospel-infused, and life-changing. Stacey has a Graduate Certificate in Women's Ministry from Heritage College and Seminary and is working toward a Graduate Certificate in Biblical Counselling.

f facebook.com/writerSWeeks

X x.com/writerSWeeks

⊙ instagram.com/writerSWeeks

You Can Make a Difference

Did you enjoy this book? You can make a difference. Honest reviews of books bring them to the attention of other readers. If you enjoyed this book, I would be grateful if you could take a few minutes to leave an online review or star rating where you purchased the book. You can also post reviews and star ratings on Goodreads and Bookbub.

www.ingramcontent.com/pod-product-compliance
Lightning Source LLC
Chambersburg PA
CBHW060441180626
46817CB00007B/2921